Dedication

This book is dedicated to those of you who support me, book after book!

May your kindle fund stay loaded, your kindle charged, your wine glass full, your mind at peace and a smile on your face.

My Gratefulness

As always, I owe all to God. Without His anointing, I would not be able to give you the books you so graciously purchase, release after release.

I will not try to list names but I must thank my husband, Willie, my children Gabrielle and Christopher. Without your sharing of me, the world would not know my name. I love you! To my family and friends who support every release, thank you.

To the many new readers and all of you who support Lakisha, THANK YOU! From the bottom of my heart, I thank you because without you purchasing, reading, reviewing and recommending; my books would never make it to be best sellers. YOU GUYS ROCK!

And to the awesomeness, who is BM Hardin, I appreciate you, more than mere words can convey. You take the time to help, others, without a second thought. I pray God will continually bless everything you do.

The Forgotten Wife

Thou Shalt Never Forget His Wife.

Rylee

"How long have you been having an affair?" Todd screams as soon as I walk through the door.

"Hello to you too," I say dropping my bags on the counter.

"How long Rylee?"

"Todd, what are you screaming about and why are you even home?"

He throws the large envelope down on the kitchen island, spilling pictures. "I'm going to ask you again, how long have you been sleeping with this dude?"

"Oh," I say when I see pictures of me in various sexual positions. Shrugging I ask, "Does it matter?"

"Yes it matters, what the hell do you mean? I find out my wife is cheating on me and you ask does it matter. Are you serious?"

"Dude, stop with all the dramatics. You know as well as I do, you haven't been in this relationship for a long time."

"Oh, so now I'm the reason you went and cheated with another man? Look at this," he says picking up a picture. "Look at it!"

"I don't need to see them, I was there but to answer your question, I didn't say you were to blame. I cheated AND I take full responsibility for it but you are not about to play the victim because you have fault too."

He laughs. "And I bet you are going to say you didn't mean to hurt me too, huh?

"I didn't-"

"No!" He yells, angrily flipping over picture after picture. "You expect me to believe you had no intentions of hurting me every time you allowed some random dude to stick his penis inside of you? Were you even thinking about my feelings each time you performed oral sex on him and then came home to kiss me?"

"If I didn't know any better, I would swear you are a devastated husband but I'm don't. And for the record, we don't kiss anymore and even if we did, I clean every part of my body before I come home."

"I'm glad you find this funny."

"It's not, trust me. However, tell me something dear husband. When was the last time we've had mind-blowing, shift your ovaries and knock your back out kind of sex like this?" I ask holding up another picture. "Tell me the last time you woke me up in the morning or hell, even put me to sleep at night."

He doesn't say anything.

"I would ask if the cat has your tongue but I already know the answer because you haven't had my cat on your tongue in," I pause. "Shit who am I kidding, I can't even remember, do you?"

"This isn't on me and you know it."

"You sure? A husband not remembering the last time he tasted a part of his wife, isn't a problem to you? A husband who doesn't care about satisfying his wife, isn't a problem? And you are shocked I cheated? Yea, okay."

"You know I've been working on opening up the new restaurant and we have a baby."

I laugh. "Um, if you haven't noticed, TJ is three and that new restaurant doesn't dismiss the fact you have a wife at home so don't give me that crap. While you are so focused on opening up your *new* restaurant," I say sarcastically, "your wife is at home, hot and horny. Baby, there is only so many times a dildo can do the job."

"You are a piece of work. What happened to you? You have never behaved like this."

"Behaved like what? Like a wife who needs my husband? All I want is to not be forgotten and for you to actually love me again!"

"You have a funny way of showing it."

"Todd, we both know I've played the happy wife for a long time but that ended when you stopped playing with me. And I have been showing you, you just never noticed."

"So, we are back to blaming this on me?"

I blow out a breath. "We can continue to have this conversation but it doesn't seem to be getting us anywhere. I made the mistake of thinking our marriage would remain happy and full of life, like it was in the beginning but I was wrong."

"I work to provide a decent living for my family!" He yells. "That should be enough to keep you from lying with some random ass dude."

"First, you need to lower your voice because I'm not yelling at you. Secondly, you aren't the only one working in this household to provide a decent living for our family yet it did not stop me from giving you what you needed, when you needed it. But as for you dear husband, you've completely said the hell with Rylee."

"No, I have not."

"I remember when you used to show up at the office and leave me breathless from orgasms or the times you'd call me to meet you somewhere for a quickie on lunch but hell, all of that has stopped. You let your restaurant business overshadow you taking care of business at home. Yes, I made a mistake but I've tried to get you to notice me, you never have time."

"Answer this one question."

"What?"

"Would you have told me had these pictures not been sent to the restaurant?" He asks.

"Nope."

Todd

"Wow. Where are you going?" I ask her.

"I'm ending this pointless conversation."

"Really, our marriage is pointless?"

"It's getting there."

She walks out the kitchen.

"Rylee, why are you breaking up our home?"

She doesn't answer as she continues into our bedroom and over to the dresser.

"Todd, have you not heard any-freaking-thing I said? See, this is part of the problem. I've tried to tell your selfish ass but you never have the time, you don't even notice me anymore."

"That's not true."

"Yes it is and you know it. Either you're running out of here first thing in the morning or coming home late at night. It is always, we'll talk later. Well, I guess this is later. Had I known pictures would get your attention, I would have sent some sooner."

"Do you care about me at all?" I ask grabbing her arm.

"Of course I do, you're my husband."

"You could have fooled me."

"Whatever Todd." She says, snatching her arm from me.

"Do you still love me?"

"Todd, I love you with ever part of me but how long do you expect me to sit by while you pay me no attention?"

"Then why haven't you apologized?"

"Oh, I definitely apologize for hurting you but when it comes to my happiness, I have no apology to give." She says heading in the bathroom with me following.

"So, what now?"

"Now, I want to take a shower in peace." She replies.

I walk away from the door and she slams it closed. I sit on the bed and after thirty minutes or so, I hear the water turn off. She opens the door but doesn't come out.

"What do you want Rylee?"

I hear her sighing before she steps to the door, her body glistening from the oil she has applied.

"Honestly Todd, I don't know. What I do know, I am tired of being unhappy."

When she walks back into the bathroom, I continue the conversation.

"Are you still sleeping with this dude?"

"No."

"How can I believe you?"

"You can believe what you want. He served the purpose I needed and that was to get your attention."

"Are you sleeping with anyone else?"

"Not at the moment."

"Seriously Rylee?"

"I am just being honest so don't ask questions you aren't ready to hear the answer too."

"You just go out and sleep with random people?"

"No but if you aren't willing to handle the business of pleasing me, I *will* get it from someone else."

"Damn."

"Why are you shocked? Do you honestly think I'm just going to sit around while you do God knows what?"

"I'm not cheating on you!" I scream.

"You could be, for all I know. Hell, if you aren't getting it from me, you must be being pleased by someone."

"Rylee, I am not cheating and I will not apologize for trying to do right by my family."

"I'm not asking you to apologize for that Todd but I am asking you to love your wife again, like you used too. You used to look at me and I would get butterflies. You used to touch me and my panties would get wet. You used to--"

"Baby, I love you."

"Yea, you just have a funny way of showing it."

She comes out of the bathroom, in her bra and panties and I look her up and down.

"Rylee, I'm sorry." I say walking over to her.

"Don't do that. Do not apologize unless you know what you're apologizing for and mean it. Don't you get it, your apology just like mine, means nothing if we aren't willing to get to the root of the problem?"

"And what is the root of the problem? I love you Rylee."

"Just because you keep saying it, doesn't make it true when you don't show it. Do I believe you love me? Yes but we both know you love your businesses more."

"That's not true."

"Todd, you get home every morning at 3AM because you never let anyone else run the new restaurant, even though you've hired capable staff members. You are gone by the time I get up and you never take a moment to even converse about anything other than our son. When was the last time you looked at me naked?" She ask spinning around.

"When did you get that tattoo on your back?"

She laughs. "I've had this tattoo for over six months and you're just now noticing but you love your wife."

When she starts to walk over to the closet, I grab her.

"Rylee, stop for a second."

"What?"

"I'm sorry I haven't been here. How can I make it up to you?" I ask kissing her.

"We can make it up to each other by choosing to fight for our marriage or letting each other go."

"Is that all?"

I kiss her again, pressing my erection on her leg.

"Yes and you thinking sex right now, is going to help our situation lets me know our problem is bigger than I thought. I'm going to start dinner."

She snatches her arm from me, goes into the closet, throwing on an oversize t-shirt and walking out.

Rylee

By the time I make it to the kitchen, Maribel, our nanny is coming through the door with TJ sleeping in her arms.

"Hey, Ms. Rylee."

"Hello Maribel, how was your day? Was he a good boy?" I ask taking him from her while she sits his bag on the counter.

"Yes ma'am, he was great as usual. I took him to the park after we ate so he is probably out for tonight."

"Great, I'll take him from here and I'll see you in the morning. Thank you so much."

"Thank you Ms. Rylee. Good night."

I try to wake TJ for a bath but he will not budge so I undress him and put him in his pajamas, resigned to bathe him in the morning. Once he is settled in his bed, I go back to the kitchen to prepare dinner. I open the refrigerator and there isn't much to choose from.

Sighing I close the door.

"Todd, I'm going to run out to pick up something to eat. Maribel just left and TJ is asleep in his room." I tell him when I walk back into the bedroom to put on pants.

"I'll go. What do you have a taste for?"

"It doesn't matter."

"Ok, I'll call Roman and get him to fix us something."

"Who is Roman?"

"My new head chef at Lilies 2."

"I didn't know you hired someone new. What happened to David?"

"I thought I told you. David moved to Houston last month."

"Yea, well I guess we are both good at keeping secrets."

I head back downstairs and stop by the kitchen to get my phone before going into my office. Sitting at the desk, I open up my computer to put the finishing touches on next month's publication for the magazine.

I'm preoccupied and my thoughts are all over the place so I decide to call my sister Raegan.

"What's up chick," she says answering.

"Hey girl, are you busy?"

"Not for you."

"You will not believe what I came home too."

"Todd buck naked in the middle of the living room floor." She laughs.

"Hell no, I wish."

"Then tell me he surprised you with something good."

"Oh, it was definitely a surprise. Todd was holding pictures of me, having sex."

"Wait, what? You having sex with who?"

"Someone I know."

She gets quiet.

"Rae?"

"Sister, please tell me you did not cheat on your husband?"

"I can't." I say sighing.

"And Todd has pictures?"

"Yes."

I hear her slamming on brakes.

"Rae, are you alright? Rae!"

"Shoot! I almost ran into the back of this truck." She exhales. "Rylee, please tell you're joking."

"I would not joke about this."

"Who sent the pictures?"

"I don't know."

"I can't you with. I'm coming over."

"You—hello?"

I look at the phone and see she's hung up.

I lay the phone down and open up Facebook. Since it's the first time I have logged in today, it has my "On this Day" memories on the top.

I click on the button and when I begin scrolling, I start to cry looking at pictures of when Todd and I were happy.

"What happened to us?" I question the air.

I slam the computer closed just as the doorbell rings.

Opening the door, Raegan doesn't say anything before pulling me into a hug which causes me to cry even harder.

"Why do you always have this effect on me?" I ask when she finally releases me.

"It's the God in me."

She closes the door and follows me into the living room.

"How did you get here so fast?"

"I was leaving a meeting, not far from here and with the mess you have going on, I know it was God ordained. Now, what is happening with you?"

"I don't know Rae."

"That's not a valid answer Rylee. You're a grown woman who runs an upscale magazine which sells thousands of copies monthly. I know you can do better than that sorry excuse for an answer."

"Please don't preach to me."

"I am not preaching but this is me prying." She says sitting on the couch. "Now talk."

I sit next to her but don't say anything.

"Don't get quiet now because clearly things are bad enough for you to cheat."

"It was the only way I could get his attention."

"That's a lie. You allowed yourself to be used by the enemy. Own your shit Rylee."

I look at her.

"What? I still have a few cuss words in my vocabulary and it is obvious you need them."

"Rae, you don't understand. Today was the first time Todd has been home, this early, in almost a year. And he only came because he got the pictures at his job. Hell, had they come here, he never would have noticed them."

"Dang girl, I didn't know your marriage had gotten this bad."

"Apparently, neither did my husband but that's because he never takes the time to listen. I'm tired of trying to get him to notice me and if those pictures got his attention, so be it."

"Why didn't you come to me?"

"I don't need counselling, I need my husband."

"And you thought cheating was the best course of action? Rylee you are better than this."

"What else was I supposed to do? All I want is for him to love me again?"

"This wasn't the way to go about that and you know it. The bible shares-"

"Rae, I don't want to hear your holy talk." I say getting up.

"That's part of your problem. You've stopped trusting God."

"I haven't, I just don't have time for church right now."

"And look how things are. Big sister, I wouldn't be who I am if I didn't offer you God, especially during a time like this. Do you not realize an unhappy home is a feeding ground for the enemy? Why do you think it was so easy for you to cheat on your husband?"

"I cheated because I had too."

"And what would you have done had you ended up pregnant or with a disease?"

"I don't know."

"Yes you do!" She says getting a little louder. "Cut the BS Rylee because this is not you and it surely is not the way you handle problems in your marriage."

"You don't understand."

"Hush and let me pray for you."

Todd

I walk into the kitchen and I hear voices. I sit the food down on the table and head into the living room.

"And God, I need you to cleanse this house. Remove anything that is not like you. We trust you God and ask your will be done. Restore this marriage and give strength to heal what our fleshly mind cannot understand. Pour peace into the parts of Rylee and Todd that are being consumed with confusion. Destroy anything that seeks to hinder and pull apart what you have joined together. In your name we pray. Amen." Raegan says.

I roll my eyes.

Rylee takes a step back and wipe her eyes. When she sees me, she jumps.

"Todd, you scared the crap out of me. I didn't hear you come in."

"Hey brother." Raegan says giving me a hug. "You are just in time."

"In time for what?" I ask. "I don't need prayer, your sister does."

"Whatever Todd." Rylee states.

"Wow." Raegan says looking from me to her sister. "It is apparent you and Rylee need to decide on a date to come and talk to me. *Together*." She emphasize.

"Ra--"

"You are coming." She says cutting Rylee off.

"For what? We both know Todd isn't going to show."

"You don't know that. Raegan, I will make time." I interject causing Rylee to look at me.

"Great. Then it's settled." She pulls out her phone. "Um, how about Monday? I don't normally have office hours but I will make an exception. Meet me at the church, let's say about 3:30."

"I'll be there."

"Rylee?"

"Fine, I'll be there."

When she is done, I walk her outside and then return to see Rylee pulling plates from the cabinet.

"Babe, can we talk?" I ask.

"Sure."

"Look, I am sorry for not being what you needed. It still doesn't excuse the fact you cheated but I am willing to forgive and forget."

"You are willing to forgive and forget?" She laughs. "Gee, thanks."

"What? I think I am being generous."

"Todd, my cheating isn't the problem and you know it. Had it not been for those pictures, we both know you wouldn't even be here right now."

"You might be right but I am, so that should count for something."

"Count for something? Are we keeping score? You are never here Todd. You never have time for your wife but you being here should count for something. Well, newsflash, it doesn't."

"Rylee, I am trying to be patient and not go off but you constantly using my work as an excuse to you cheating is wearing thin. Sure, I work a lot but it did not give you the right to cheat. You took vows for better and for worse."

"So did you!"

"I haven't broken my vows ma'am."

"YOU DID!" She yells. "You broke your vows to love, cherish and honor me. Each time you walk out of here without telling me you love me, you break your vows. Every time we go days without speaking, you break your vows. When I have to find affection in the arms of someone else because my husband is too busy, you break your vows. So, stop acting like I am the only one who has a part in destroying this marriage boo."

"And I have apologized for my part. What more do you want from me?"

"FOR YOU TO STOP FORGETTING ME AND LOVE ME AGAIN!"

"Dammit Rylee, I do love you and you ought to know that."

"How Todd? How am I supposed to know when you will not show me?"

"I do show you!" I say getting angry. "By working to ensure we have everything we need. You're not homeless or hungry, you drive whatever car you want, you shop when you feel like it and you have a shoe closet with over 300 pairs of shoes."

"I don't need your money."

"What about the fact I haven't said anything about the ten pounds you have put on."

She looks at me as tears slide down her face.

"Oh, now you cry. You're the one who cheated sweetheart, not me so you don't get to cry your way out of this. You were wrong Rylee and if I have to worry about what my wife is doing every time I'm at work then maybe--"

"Maybe what?"

"Never mind. Let's just eat."

"No thank you. I've lost my appetite."

Rylee

Standing in line at the coffee shop, on Monday morning, someone taps me on the shoulder. At first I ignore it but they tap again.

I turn.

"I apologize for bothering you but you look familiar, have we meet before?"

"It's a possibility." I reply, turning back around.

"Did you graduate from Houston High School?"

"Nope."

"What church do you attend?"

"I don't."

"Do we work together?"

"Nope, I'm pretty sure we don't," I say smiling to keep from getting upset.

"How can you be so sure? I work for a very large corporation." He says, smiling back.

"Seeing that I work for myself, I'm 100% sure so what can I do for you sir?"

"My bad," he says holding up his hands. "You just look so familiar."

I smile as I move up, getting ready to order my white chocolate mocha.

"Well my name is Al and I would love to buy your coffee."

"Thanks Al but I'm capable of buying my own. How about I buy yours, what are you having?"

His eyes widen.

"Do you have a problem with a woman buying your drink?"

"No, uh, no but it's kind of weird. An average woman would be expecting me to buy hers."

"Well Al, I am not your average woman."

"I see."

"Now, would you like me to buy your drink or not?"

"Sure," he replies.

He orders his drink and I place mine before paying.

"Would you care to join me?" He asks.

"No thanks, I have a meeting to get too."

"Oh, what do you do?"

"I am the founder of Truth Magazine. Have you heard of it?"

"Yes, I've seen it while in line at the grocery store."

"Well Al, now I expect you to get a subscription." I say handing him a card with the magazine's information. He opens his mouth to say something but the barista calls my name. "It was nice meeting you Al. Take care."

"Rylee."

I turn when I hear someone call my name.

"Liam, what are you doing here?"

"I was hoping to catch you."

"Why?"

"You haven't been answering my calls?"

"There is a reason for that. Now, if you'll excuse me."

"Are you really going to walk away like I'm not trying to have a conversation?"

"Liam, are you really going to do this here, after what you did?" I ask while looking around.

"All I'm trying to do is get you to talk to me."

I grab his arm and pull him outside. "You knew what this was in the beginning but for you to send pictures to my husband was low."

"Pictures? I didn't send anything to your husband."

"Stop lying, who else could have?"

"Rylee baby--"

"Do not baby me. I made it perfectly clear this was only a one night stand. Why are you making it into a problem?"

"It isn't a problem unless you make it one."

"What is that supposed to mean?"

"Look, I like you and I want to continue to see you."

"That's not happening. I'm married and so are you."

"That didn't stop us previously."

"Wow."

"All I want is a chance to spend more time with you, Rylee."

I walk closer to him. "You are a grown ass man who I spent three hours with, a month ago. I only did it for the sake of getting my husband's attention. There is nothing more between us so go home, work or wherever you are headed."

"I can't help it. You're intoxicating."

"And so is alcohol. Here," I reach into my purse and pull out a fifty dollar bill. "Go to the nearest liquor store, buy you something strong to drink and leave me the hell alone."

"You can't do me like this!"

I get in my car and drive off. Pulling the phone from my purse, I dial a number.

"Hey, we may have a problem."

I make it to the office to find Natalie and Raul waiting at the door. They are in a heated discussion so I don't even stop to acknowledge it. I head into my office but before I can even get my jacket off, they both come running in.

"Whoa, what's going on?"

"Tell her!" Natalie says.

"Tell me what?"

"You've got to read this email that came in last night." Raul says sliding me his iPad.

Dear Editor-in-Chief of Truth Magazine,

My name, for the purpose of this email, is Sampson and I am writing because I need some advice. I am married and although I love my wife, I've seem to have forgotten her. I didn't mean too but life got busy and in the way.

We rarely spend time together anymore and we haven't had sex in months. Recently, I found out she had an affair and I cannot bring myself to forgive her. I know I am the reason she found comfort in the arms of another man but she should have talked to me about it and not cheated. That was a low blow.

Please help me because I am so confused, angry and ready to pack my shit.

Sincerely,

Sampson

"Okay." I say looking up at Raul and Natalie who are waiting like children expecting a cookie.

"Okay? Is that all you got?"

"What else am I supposed to say?"

"Rylee, this could be May's featured article." Raul says.

"Maybe."

"Maybe, girl, I mean Rylee, this can cause all kinds of buzz for us. Think about it."

"I am thinking and I think it will be a lot of work."

"But we can pull it off. We run this email along with a response, every month until there is a resolution."

"Yeah," Natalie says. "If we do that, it'll make our readers eager for the next issue."

"And we create an online blog, linked to Truth's website."

"I don't know. It seems like a lot of extra work. Besides, how do we know he will even respond?"

"Girl, I mean Rylee. I'm sorry, I'm excited but with this subject, we can expect hundreds of responses so if he doesn't we will go with somebody else."

"What will we call it though?"

"The Forgotten Wife." They both say together.

"I don't know. Who is going to respond?"

"You." Natalie answers.

"Now stop tripping, open that computer and respond to this man."

"Why do I have to respond? You read the email first, you respond."

"I'm not the editor-in-chief and you are the only wife in the office. If this is tailor made to anybody, it's you."

"If I do, the both of you will need to come up with a marketing campaign and design for the layout."

"Don't worry about that. You let us handle our jobs while you handle yours."

"Fine. Now, get out of my office." When they start to walk out, I remember the meeting with my sister. "Oh Natalie, I need you to clear my schedule for the afternoon. I have a meeting at 3:30 I cannot get out of."

"Okay. Anything else?"

"Yeah, has Mario called about this month's issue? Were there any printing problems?"

"No, as of right now everything is on schedule."

"Great. What about the Save the Date invitations to Truth's Anniversary Party?"

"An email blast went out this morning and it has been uploaded to the website."

"Thank you Natalie."

"No problem."

When she leaves, I sit down at my desk to pull up this email.

"The Forgotten Wife." I say out loud. Tapping my finger on the keypad, I decide, what the heck."

To: Sampson

Subject: RE: The Forgotten Wife

Dear Sampson,

While I will never condone cheating, can I ask you a question? What right do you have to be angry at your wife when you said yourself, you've forgotten her? I am willing to bet she tried to talk to you but "life has gotten busy and in the way" and you never noticed. Tell me, dear husband, how much longer did you expect your wife to sit idle while she was being forgotten?

Signed,

A Forgotten Wife.

I close the laptop and realize I'd gotten upset.

"This isn't about you Rylee."

I get up and walk around the office to take a few deep breaths.

When I am calm, I go back over to my desk to start my day. I have a lot to get through before I need to leave.

I finish going through emails, approving items for next month's issue and finalizing plans for Truth's fifth anniversary gala. I look at my watch and realize it's after eleven and I have paper everywhere. As I try to clean some of it up, my phone rings.

Looking under the mound of paper I finally find it.

Whose number is this?

"This is Rylee." I answer.

"So you leave me standing in the middle of a coffee shop parking lot without even a second glance?"

"What do you want Liam?"

"I want to talk to you."

"There's nothing for us to talk about."

Natalie buzzes.

"Can we just meet for drinks?"

"Liam, lose my number."

I press the end button.

"Rylee, your husband is on line one."

I roll my eyes and pick up the phone. "Let me guess, you're calling to cancel?"

"I'm sorry but I cannot make the meeting with your sister."

"Figures."

"Look, I had every intention on being there but I had a mix up with a huge delivery I need for a party we're hosting and I've got to take care of it. You know--"

I hang up on him and call my sister.

She doesn't even say hello.

"Rylee Abigail Winston-Patrick, I know you are not about to cancel on me?"

"Todd can't make it."

"So, what about you?"

"What's the point? This was supposed to be about us fixing our marriage and if he can't get away for an hour then it's obvious I am not his priority."

"Don't talk like that. You know Todd loves you."

"That's the thing Raegan, I don't and I am tired of waiting for him to show it."

"Rylee, don't do anything stupid."

"I'm not about to do anything stupid but I am going to do something about my sanity and that's asking my husband for a divorce. I'll talk to you later."

Todd

"Boss, you know I can handle this if you need to leave." Roman says.

"Nah, I got it."

"Are you sure? You said the meeting was important."

"Yea but right now, my business is more important. I'll deal with the other later."

I feel my phone vibrate. When I turn it over and see Raegan's number, I press ignore. After a few seconds, she sends a text.

HER: Stop ignoring me. You're messing up big brother.

ME: I know and I'll make it up.

HER: You better before it's too late.

--knock on the door—

"Boss, are you busy?"

"Yea." I say without looking up.

"Are you sure?"

When I hear the door close, I look up to see my Sous Chef, Octavia. She slowly walks toward me, undoing her chef jacket.

"What are you doing?" I ask her.

"Um, you look a little stress."

"No, we can't do this. Roman is here."

"Then you'll need to keep me quiet."

She sits on my desk, spreading her legs in front of me allowing me to smell the fruity body oil she knows I like.

"Why don't you have on any panties?"

"I didn't think I'd need them."

I stand up from my chair just as Roman buzzes from the kitchen.

"Todd, did you finish the list of things we need from the store? I'm about to go out."

I push away from her and press the button.

"Yeah, I'll meet you up front with the list and card."

She pulls me back with her leg.

"Stop. Get down and fix your clothes."

"Come on, I only need five minutes." She purrs.

"I can't and we've got to stop this."

"Why? I thought you liked this."

She grabs me and cover my mouth with hers.

"No, we've got to stop."

"Three minutes." She says taking my hand and rubbing between her legs.

"Hmm. No, I cannot risk getting caught. I have enough problems at home as it is."

"Boo, that can be easily remedied if you moved out."

"You know I am not about to leave my son."

"I hate to be the bearer of bad news sweetie but you've already left your son."

"What is that supposed to mean?"

"Come on Todd, we both know you are no Dad of The Year. When was the last time you were at home to give him a bath or put him to bed? He's what, two or three and probably barely knows you. You moving out will not shatter him."

"So you're an expert on marriage and family now?"

"No but I am expert on you."

"Octavia please. We both know you're nothing but a good stress reliever."

"At least I stand in my truth. What about you? Weren't you supposed to be going to a meeting to fix your marriage but instead you're here?" She laughs.

"My marriage is none of your concern!"

"You sure because I know the number of nights you spend in my bed and they overshadow the number of nights you've been home."

"Get out of my office!"

"Truth hurts huh?" She stands and fixes her clothes. "It's okay. I'll see you tonight boo."

"Hey, are you alright?" Roman asks standing at the door.

"My bad man, here's the card and the list. If there is anything else you can think of, get it."

"Todd," he says coming in and closing the door. "I don't mean to get in your personal business--"

"Then don't."

"I don't mean to get in your personal business but fooling around with Octavia is a disaster waiting to happen."

I look at him.

"Oh, did you think it was a secret?"

"Whether I did or didn't, what I do is none of your business."

"Look man, if you value your marriage, you'll leave that chick alone because she's not worth it. Trust me, I've been in your shoes and losing my wife was the worst mistake of my life."

"Wait, aren't you married now?"

"I am but it is my second marriage. The first one, I allowed to end because I was like you, willingly putting any and everything before her. She even put my stuff on the lawn, changed the locks and I still didn't get it. You know what did, seeing her with another man. A man who did all the things she begged me to do because I had forgotten her."

"I haven't forgotten my wife, I'm busy running two restaurants that takes care of her. If she cannot understand that, so be it."

"Where does Octavia fit in because I am pretty sure she isn't part of the business?"

"Roman, you let me worry about my marriage while you worry about keeping a job. I know what I'm doing."

"You're right, my bad but don't say I didn't warn you."

"I don't need your warning, I got this."

"Okay. I'll be back in an hour to prep for tonight's dinner service."

Rylee

I pack up my things as I get ready to head out. I'd already taken the afternoon off so I may as well utilize it.

"Natalie, I'm heading out. Call me if you need me."

"Wait," Raul hollers. "Did you hear back from the dude?"

"No yet. He probably will not respond."

"I think he will." Natalie says. "He sounds desperate."

"Not desperate enough to notice his wife, apparently."

"He's going to respond." Raul says. "I just know it and when he does, we're going to sell millions of copies."

"Calm down boy wonder." I say laughing. "If he does, we will have to come up with a better way to develop this story to be a win for all of us. Maybe some kind of teaser or way to get this out to the public."

"Hold on." Raul says. "Maybe we can have an unveiling at the anniversary party, then a full media blitz."

"That's a great idea because it will create chatter among social media." Natalie says. "We need to come up with some marketing sketches."

"Why don't the both of you work on that while I'll jot down some ideas I have swirling in my head and we can discuss tomorrow. How about breakfast?"

"Sounds good. Our usual, Perkins Restaurant?"

"Yes, let's say nine."

"See you then."

Getting to the car, my phone rings. I press ignore. It rings again.

"Liam, I asked you to stop calling me. Whatever this could have been ended when my husband received those pictures."

"Baby please, listen to me. I did not send those pictures."

"Whatever. Goodbye."

"Why are you acting like you don't need what I have?"

"I don't."

"Of course you do because we both know your husband is lacking in that area."

"You know nothing about my husband."

"I know I needed to fill in where he was falling short."

I chuckle. "Oh, so you think giving me one orgasm entitles you to take my husband's place?"

"Stop acting like you don't remember how I made you feel. If memory serves me right, it was my name you were moaning and not your husband's. And we both know it was more than one orgasm."

"What's your point?"

He laughs. "Woman, stop being stubborn and let me rock your world."

"I can't."

"Let me put my tongue in all the places that makes you squirm." His voice now sounding seductive.

"Liam, I can't."

"Let me make your insides shake while I slide your toes into my mouth. Then you can go home and think about me when you're in bed, tonight, by yourself."

I don't say anything.

"Your eyes are closed and you want to touch yourself, don't you?"

A small moan slips pass my lips.

"Touch yourself baby."

I bite my lip, although he can't see it.

"Meet me at the same place we were last time. I'll text you the room number." He says hanging up.

I lay my head on the headrest.

A few seconds later, my phone dings.

LIAM: Room 320

I stare at the message before throwing the phone into the passenger seat and starting the car.

Twenty minutes later, I am standing outside the door. I raise my hand to knock but it opens.

"You came."

Moving back to let me in, I drop my purse on the couch and fall next to it.

"Only because I need your help." I exhale, loudly. "Rae, I almost slept with Liam again. I have the room number in my text message and I almost went."

"What stopped you?"

"He's not who I want." I say getting angry. "I want my husband. Rae, what am I doing wrong?"

"Girl, don't you dare take the blame for someone else. You know, as well as I do, you cannot make someone be who and what you need. It has to be their choice, especially in a marriage."

"But we used to be happy. He used to love me and it showed by the way he looked at me. Now he barely glances in my direction. He never even noticed the tattoo I've had on my back, for over six months."

"Do you think he's having an affair?"

"To be honest, the thought never crossed my mind but if he's not being satisfied sexually by me, he has to be getting it from somewhere."

"What are you going to do?"

"Isn't that what I have you for? To give me some Godly advice."

"The Godly advice is to work on your marriage, giving all of you until you know, without a shadow of a doubt your work is in vain. However, the sisterly advice, roll up on his ass and give him a beat down."

"Whoa Mickey Tyson." I laugh.

"Rylee, in all seriousness, marriage is not about one person working to make it last but it is a covenant between two people who have now become one in everything. And when one isn't pulling their share of the load, the other suffers. Think about a bicycle. Can you ride it without two wheels? No because it needs both to move forward. What I am saying, either repair the wheel or ditch the bike."

"Thank you baby sister. You are such a profound preacher to be so young."

"Girl, I am 38 years old and I've been in ministry for over ten years but I didn't read on how to make a marriage work. Nathan and I have gone through a few things."

"Yea right. Nathan would never cheat on you."

"Who said anything about it being Nathan?"

My mouth falls open.

"Raegan, you old--"

"Don't you dare, this is God's house."

"You cheated on Nathan?"

"It's not something I am proud of but it was early in my ministry career when we weren't on the same page. Shoot, we weren't even in the same book. He couldn't understand why I was changing and I couldn't understand why he wasn't. All of my focus was on God and the church and I spent all my extra time doing something related to ministry."

"Oh, I know."

"I had tunnel vision and my husband was nowhere in the vicinity. I guess I was angry at him for not being more open to the change that was happening with me. I started spending time with another man who was also in ministry. I thought he understood me and one night, we slept together."

"And you told your husband?"

"I had too because it took me making that mistake to realize, that man wasn't who I wanted nor needed. I needed my husband."

"How did you repair it?"

"He forgave me and we made a vow to put it behind us and never bring it up again. Understand, it wasn't easy because it took Nathan a while to forget but we made it and it took both of us being willing. Our marriage wouldn't have survived with just one of us trying."

"Wow, well I'll be damn!"

"RYLEE!"

"I am just so outdone. I never would have thought, you would cheat."

"Honey, we all have a past."

"I see."

"Now, you have to decide what you want to do but do me one favor."

"What's that?"

"Give it thirty days."

"Thirty what?"

"Rylee, it is just a month and during that time, come back to church and rekindle your romance with God."

"I don't know Raegan."

"Think about it."

"I will."

"You promise?" She asks.

"I promise."

"So, I'll see you Sunday?"

"I guess."

Todd

I walk into the kitchen of the restaurant at the same time Rylee is coming through the back door.

"Rylee, what are you doing here?"

"I need to talk to you and since this seems to be where you're spending all of your time, I thought I'd stop by. Do you have a moment?"

"I know you're upset about me blowing you off earlier but there really was a disaster I had to fix."

"There is always a disaster when it comes to this place but I did not come to argue, I came to talk. Do you have a moment or not?"

"I do. Would you like something to eat?"

She looks at me but I grab her hand before she has a chance to object, leading her over to the chef's table.

"Good evening ma'am, what can I get you to eat?"

"Rylee this my head chef, Roman. Roman this is my wife Rylee."

"It's nice to finally meet you Ramon. I'll take a ribeye with asparagus and mac & cheese."

"What about you, boss?"

"I'm good."

When Roman walks away, Rylee looks at me.

"What?"

"This is awkward and sad, at the same time. I don't know the last time we've actually sat down together. Does that not bother you?"

"Babe, I know I've been busy a lot lately but I plan on cutting back my hours and giving Roman more room to lead."

"How many times have I heard this knowing--"

"You must be the Mrs." Octavia says interrupting us.

"I am and you are?"

"Oh, your husband didn't tell you. I'm his, I mean I'm his Sous Chef. The name is Octavia." She smirks, extending her hand.

"Well, I hope you are as great at your job as you are interrupting."

"Oh I am. Right boss?"

"Octavia, what do you need?" I ask getting agitated.

"I was going to grab you something to drink and I needed to know what she prefers since I already know what you like."

"Look--"

I place my hand on Rylee's leg to prevent her from getting up.

"Octavia, don't you have dinner requests to fill?"

"Just trying to be useful." She says winking before walking off.

"So, how long have you been sleeping with her?" Rylee asks.

"Babe, don't start because I am not sleeping with her."

"Todd, cut the BS. Even a blind person can see it and Ms. Thang makes it obvious."

"Baby, I am not sleeping with her. She's just my Sous Chef."

"If she was just your Sous Chef, why haven't you bothered to mention her?"

"I thought I did but I guess it slipped my mind."

"You've had a lot of things to slip your mind lately."

"Rylee, I know I have messed up, so have you but can we please discuss this at home? What do you want to drink?"

"Wine and bring the bottle." I reply.

"Be right back."

A few minutes later, I walk back in the kitchen to see Roman placing a plate down in front of Rylee.

"This looks and smells amazing." She says smiling at Ramon.

"He is a great cook." I say handing her a glass of wine and sitting back down. "Now, what did you want to talk about?"

"Us. Todd, things cannot-"

Octavia calls my name. I hold my hand up, signaling for her to give me a minute.

"Go ahead."

"I was saying, things--"

She calls again.

"Babe, give me a minute. I promise I'll be right back."

"Do you not see me having a conversation with my wife? What's up?" I ask Octavia.

"A few of the customers have complained about the red wine sauce for the beef wellington."

"Well fix it."

"I did but I need you to taste it for me and tell me what you think."

Unable to stop her, she lifts the spoon to my mouth.

"Uh," I say trying to catch the liquid from dropping. She reaches and wipes the corner of my mouth with her hand.

"Octavia, what are you doing?"

She doesn't get a chance to answer before a glass hits the stove, directly in the middle of us. We both jump back.

"Rylee, what the hell?"

She throws the plate of food in our direction.

"You don't even have the common decency to control your whore in my presence!"

She gets up and flings a skillet at us.

"Rylee, stop!" I say ducking from the other objects flying in my direction. "Rylee!"

Roman grabs her as some of the servers come running in.

"Mrs. Patrick, please calm down." Roman says.

"Let me go!"

"I will if you promise not to throw anything else."

"Don't worry because the only other thing I'm throwing away, this time, is my husband. Don't bother coming home."

When she storms out, I turn back to Octavia who is laughing while Roman is instructing the others to get back to work.

"What was that bullshit?"

"What?" She shrugs. "I can't help your wife is sensitive."

"Octavia, get out of my restaurant!"

"Are you serious?"

"Does it look like I'm joking?"

"Fine! I'll leave but I will be back."

Rylee

I walk in the house and I am fuming. After slamming the door, I throw my purse and keys down on the kitchen's island.

"Mrs. Rylee, are you okay?" Maribel asks running in.

"Yes Maribel, I didn't mean to scare you."

"Is everything alright? Do you need me to stay with the baby?"

"No, I got him from here. Has he had dinner yet?"

"No ma'am, I was just about to fix him something."

"I will take care of it. You go on home."

"Are you sure Mrs. Rylee? I can stay while you take a bath."

"I'm sure and I really appreciate you. I'll see you tomorrow."

She walks over and gives me a hug. "Everything will be okay Mrs. Rylee."

"Thank you Maribel."

I wait a few minutes to calm myself down. I then walk into the living room to TJ playing in the floor.

"Mommy!"

"Hey baby." I say scooping him up. "How was your day?"

"Good."

"Are you hungry?"

He shakes his head yes.

"What do you want to eat?"

"Pasta!" He says lifting both hands in the air.

I laugh. "Then pasta it is."

I take him into the kitchen and put him in the chair at the island. I grab some coloring pages and crayons from the drawer and he excitedly begins to color.

"Spaghetti or mac and cheese?"

"Mac and cheese."

I put water on for the pasta before getting the cheese, butter, milk and flour.

A few minutes later, Todd comes through the door.

"Daddy!"

"Hey little man, how are you?"

"Good."

When Todd bends down, he throws his hands around Todd's neck.

"Is mommy fixing you dinner?"

"Unha."

"Can daddy have some?"

"Unha."

I roll my eyes as Todd sits TJ back in the chair.

"You're home early. Does that mean, you didn't have anybody to occupy your time?"

"Rylee--"

"Save it Todd. I am sick of being your second, no make that third choice."

"You are not my third choice."

I laugh. "You could have fooled me with the restaurants being first and Octavia second, it's clear to me we are third."

"I am not sleeping with Octavia."

I walk close to him. "Baby, you may not be sleeping with her but you're surely screwing her."

"You got some nerve when you've been sleeping with some random dude."

"TO GET YOUR ATTENTION!"

TJ jumps.

I take a deep breath and decide to walk back to the stove. Todd comes behind me.

"Do not touch me."

"You are a piece of work. You blame me for something you have no proof of when you've been doing God knows what behind my back."

"I only slept with him once but it's obvious where you've been spending your late nights. And then for her to throw it in my face and you let her."

"I can't control a grown person."

I laugh.

"Then control your whore."

He grabs my arm and I jerk it away.

"Don't touch me."

"Mommy."

"Look, take TJ and spend some time with him while I finish his pasta before this turns into something more."

"More like what?"

"More like me throwing this hot water in your face."

"Wow, has it really come to that?"

"Yep."

"Can we finish this later?"

"No, I am finished."

Todd

After TJ is fed, I give him a bath then Rylee and I read him a bedtime story.

When we are done, Rylee walks out ahead of me while I turn out his light.

"Rylee, can we please talk?"

"About what Todd? We both know how this is going to end so let's stop going around in circles."

"Wait, are you leaving me?"

"May as well, you've already left me."

"Baby, wait, please."

She turns back to me with tears in her eyes.

"All I want is for you to notice me again."

My cell phone rings. I pull it out of my pocket and it's Octavia. I press decline.

"Rylee, I am sorry--"

My phone rings again.

Octavia.

"Go on and get that. It must be important." She says walking into the bathroom and slamming the door.

"Yea?" I say answering the phone.

"You're in a foul mood, you must be at home."

"What do you want Octavia?" I whisper while walking out the bedroom into the office.

"I need to talk to you."

"Does it have anything to do with your job?"

"Well yea, of course it does. Both of them."

"What do you mean?"

"The one at the restaurant and the one in my bed."

"Look, you no longer have to worry about filling either of those. Your blatant disrespect of my wife was--"

"My blatant disrespect? She's your wife, not mine so if anyone is being disrespectful, it is you boo."

"You're right and because of that I cannot continue to allow you to work at a business we both own."

She laughs. "You know you cannot just fire me, right?"

"Yes I can because Tennessee is an at-will state, which means I can terminate employment at any time and without a reason. So consider yourself terminated and I will mail your last check."

"We will see."

"What does that mean?"

"Hashtag me too." She laughs again.

"Are you trying to blackmail me?"

"No boo, I am only looking out for me. We both know you slept with me and when I cut it off, you fired me."

"Oh, is that the story you're going with?"

"Yep, unless you and I can come to some sort of arrangement."

"What kind of arrangement?"

"You continue to meet my needs."

"And what needs are those?"

"All of them." She coos.

"This sure sounds like blackmail to me."

"You can call it what you like but I call it business."

"Business huh? Well, find somebody else because my services are no longer available."

"Then I'll see you in court."

"Good luck with that."

I hang up. When I turn to walk out, Rylee is standing there with her arms folded.

"It sounds like you have a mess on your hand."

I can't say anything.

"What happened to us?" She questions.

"I don't know." I say sitting on the couch. "Life got in the way, I guess."

"No, I think you forgot you had a wife."

"That's not true Rylee and you know it."

"It is true Todd. When was the last time you held me, kissed me or made love to me?"

"I don't know."

"When was the last time we actually held a conversation or fell asleep watching a movie?"

"I don't know."

"When was the last time we went out on a date or cooked dinner together?"

"I.DON'T.KNOW."

"When was the last--"

"Damn, I get it!"

"No you don't get it. You have a woman, working in our business who can probably tell me what my husband had for dinner yesterday because I do not know. Hell, maybe she can tell me how you taste because I can't remember that either. So forgive me sweetie but you clearly don't get it."

I open my mouth to counter her argument but I have nothing to say in defense because she's right.

"And here I am, being a fool because I think, surely my husband will realize what he's been missing after seeing those pictures. Just maybe, my husband would see how desperate I am for his touch and he'd come home. Instead, you can care less."

"I do care."

"No you don't. You're upset because you didn't think I had the courage to cheat. In fact, you are more upset the pictures went to your job more than you are at the thought of me cheating.

"That is not true." I say standing up.

"It is. You want to know the part that hurts the most? The very thing I've been wanting, you've been giving to someone else. How's that for a slap in the face?"

"Sex, is that all you want?"

"No Todd, the one thing I want is you but thank you for confirming what I already know."

"What's that?"

"Your relationship with Octavia."

"What else do you want from me?"

"You asking that very question, again, lets me know I only need one more thing from you."

"What's that?"

"A divorce."

Rylee

Sunday morning, I get up early to prepare for church. When I am done getting myself and TJ dressed, I grab my purse and keys to head out.

"Hey, where are y'all off too?" Todd asks.

I don't answer.

"Rylee, you didn't hear me ask you a question?" I ask standing in front of her.

"Todd, leave me alone please."

"I just asked a simple question."

"And I gave you a simple answer, now move."

"Tell your boyfriend I said hello."

"I will."

I push pass him. Getting to the car, I put TJ in his car seat before I get in and pull out of the garage.

Making it to Zion Temple Church, I pray I am able to talk to Raegan prior to service.

I park, grab TJ and my things and walk inside. Raegan is coming out of her office when I round the corner.

"Rylee, you came!" She says pulling me into a hug. "Oh my God."

"Do not cry. I am not playing Rae."

"I'm not," she says sniffing. "I am just so happy to see you."

TJ pulls on her dress.

"Hey auntie's boo!" She scoops him up, squeezing him causing him to laugh. "Y'all come into my office."

We follow her inside where she sits TJ on the couch.

"Rylee, seriously, I am happy you came."

"To be honest, I almost didn't come but I am tired and trying to do it on my own isn't working. My back is against the wall."

"Rylee, you do know God is not moved by your desperation, right? I understand you want guidance but don't make God your last option."

"If I can't turn to God then why am I here?"

"That is not what I mean. Look, many times we come to God when we are desperate and in need of Him to move swiftly but He doesn't work that way. If He did, a lot of us would be receiving things our flesh isn't ready or capable of handling. And although you've made the effort, by coming to church today, it doesn't mean your marriage will be fixed by the time you get home or all your problems solved. In fact, the enemy is going to work overtime because he needs to discourage you from trusting God, especially now. But you made the first step and it is my prayer you find new hope to keep pushing. It will not be easy but will you at least try?"

I nod.

"And will you talk to me when you feel like giving up?"

"I feel like giving up." I say crying.

She comes and sits next to me. "Talk to me."

"He's been having an affair."

"Oh sister."

I lay my head on her shoulder.

"I'm tired Rae."

"Do you remember when I asked you to give it thirty days?"

"Yes."

"I still need you to do that."

I raise up and look at her.

"Did you not hear what I just said?"

"Yes but you also cheated Rylee."

"I know but--"

"There is no but. Will you do this for me?" She asks.

"What's the point?"

"Obedience."

"Obedience? Are you serious?"

"Yep. Obedience is better than sacrifice."

Forty-five minutes later, Raegan stands at the podium and takes her text. She is preaching on the story of Hagar in Genesis chapter sixteen.

"There are some of you, in here, who have been questioning God a lot lately. You feel alone, like nobody has your back. You've tried to do it yourself but it isn't working. You've tried to remain faithful but you keep having to fight off attack after attack.

You try to smile but the very act of suicide is plaguing your thoughts. You try to tune them out but every time it gets quiet, you hear them again. You try to sleep your way out of the funk but each night when you close your eyes, you are tormented by the nightmares.

And some of you are just like Hagar, finding yourself in the wilderness because you had to run from the very thing that promised to do right by you. You're just like Hagar, in the wilderness because the person who was supposed to take care of you, cast you out.

You're in the wilderness because the ones you thought had your back let you fall. But I am glad you showed up this morning because God told me to tell you, there is a promise right there in the wilderness."

"Preach!" Someone yells out.

"Amen Pastor!"

I am staring at her, in shock because it feels like she is preaching directly to me. Did she know I would show up this morning?

Nah, she could have known. Could she?

Raegan continues, "Beloved, you're in the wilderness and it has you thinking about doing some strange things. You're in the wilderness and he has you contemplating doing some stuff you wouldn't normally do but I need you to wait.

Yes ma'am, yes sir; before you plot that revenge, wait. Before you try to make that person pay for forgetting you, hold on a minute. See, this wilderness is not about the one who cast you out but it's for your sake. This wilderness experience is testing your obedience to what you heard from God. And when you are obedient, the promise of God can be yours.

For just like Hagar, God is sending you back to the place or person who has caused you pain and shame. However, it is not to punish you but to test your obedience in Him. All you need to do is return, submit and shut up.

Here's where you get your hope. God is saying, when you obey me, the reward of your pain will be increased in such a way, it'll be too big for you to formalize into words. Beloved, wherever your wilderness is, God can meet you there but you need to be obedient to His word and if He didn't tell you to leave, go back.

Whatever it is, God has told or shown you; be obedient because obedience is better than sacrifice. And God rewards your obedience."

Raegan continues to preach as I sit there listening, hanging on to her every word.

After service, I pick TJ up from children's church and head back to Raegan's office to wait for her. She comes in followed by her husband.

"Wow Rae. I can't even put into words how powerful your message was."

"Thank you sister. I couldn't figure out why God led me in that direction until you walked in this morning. Thank you for being obedient."

She hugs me.

Releasing me, Nathan pulls me into another hug. "Rylee, it is so good to see you. How have you been?"

"I've been okay, what about you Nathan?"

"I am great. Are you coming home to Zion Temple?"

"Um, I'm thinking about it."

"We miss you around here and we'd love to have you back."

"Don't run her off babe." Rae says slapping his arm.

"He's fine and I am truly thinking about it."

He gives me a thumbs up before turning to Rae. "I'm headed to my meeting with the deacon board. You know it can run over so go on and eat without me."

She kisses him goodbye.

When he leaves, Rae and I decide to grab some lunch. Walking out to my car, I see a note on the windshield. I get it and stick it in my purse before putting TJ in his seat.

While waiting for my sister to come out, I open the envelope to see a picture of Todd asleep with his head on a woman's chest. I turn it over to read what is written on the back.

"While you are in service, pray for your husband to stay at home and out of my bed."

Todd

I hear the garage going up so I meet Rylee at the door. I walk out and get TJ, who is sleeping, from his seat.

"Hey, how was church?" I ask Rylee, walking in behind her.

"Can you lay him down so we can talk?"

"Sure."

I take him into his room and come back into the kitchen.

"Are you hungry?"

"No, I had lunch with Raegan. Here." She says.

"What's this?"

"It was on my windshield when I came out of church."

My mouth falls open.

"Rylee--"

"Look Todd, I don't want another apology but I am tired of being on this merry-go-round of mess. I realize I cannot make you change or be who I need you to be and I am sorry for ever thinking I could."

"What are you saying? Do you really want a divorce?"

"I do but I promised Raegan I would give it thirty days."

"Thirty days and then what?"

"Then we figure out what's next."

"After all these years, our marriage has come down to a probationary period?"

"That's all I have the strength to give."

I laugh.

"What's funny?"

"You go to church one time and come home acting like you're holier than thou. You are no angel Rylee."

"I didn't say I was but what are we doing Todd? What is this? Neither of us are happy and you know it."

"Whatever Rylee."

"Why are you so upset? Can you honestly say this marriage has been a priority to you?"

"No but I am trying to fix it."

"How? Last I checked, you are screwing the help and I'm the one being harassed and embarrassed. The least you can do is keep her on a leash and away from your wife."

"Just tell me what you want?"

"I want some space to figure this out. Can you give me that?"

"Fine! If space is what you want then space is what you will get."

I storm out of the house and jump into my truck, headed straight to Octavia's house.

By the time I pull into the driveway and get out, she meets me at the door.

"What's up boo? What do I owe this visit?"

"Why would you put this picture on my wife's car?" I question, throwing it at her.

"What are you talking about?"

She bends down and picks it up.

"I don't know what other chick you're sleeping with but this is not me."

"Stop lying! Who else could it be?"

"That's for you to find out but since you're here." She says stepping back to let her robe open.

I grab her by the throat, pushing her further into the house.

"This is not a joke. Why are you messing with my family?"

When I release her, she slides down on the floor crying.

"What is wrong with you?" She asks rubbing her throat.

"Leave my family alone."

I turn to walk away but she grabs my leg.

"All I want is you Todd and I know you want me."

I push her away. "NO I DON'T! Stay away from my family."

Walking out to my truck, I hear her screaming.

"TODD YOU CANNOT LEAVE ME!"

I get into my truck and pull off, deciding to go to my first restaurant instead of Lilies 2 because I knew if Octavia decided, she'd go there.

It is ran by the general manager and head chef, Logan who isn't all up in my business like Ramon.

I surprise him when I walk in.

"Hey Todd, were we supposed to meet today?"

"No, I am just here to take care of some things. I will be in the office but I do not want to be disturb."

"Yes sir."

I go in and slam the door before beginning to pace.

"Think Todd. You've got to fix this." I say talking to myself. My phone vibrates, in my pocket but I don't bother to answer it. It continues to throb against my leg so I remove it and see its Octavia. I press decline and block her number.

I go over to the computer at the desk. Once it powers on, I bring up the internet to search for restraining order procedures and nanny cams.

My phone vibrates with a text from an unknown number.

Text: "You cannot get rid of me that easy but if you want to play, let us play. Be warned, you may not like the outcome. -- O."

My reply: "Octavia, leave me alone. PLEASE!"

Text: "My pleasure."

Rylee

The next morning I walk into the office to find Raul pacing.

"What's up with you?" I ask.

"Are you serious? Did dude respond?"

"Shoot, I haven't checked. I've had so much going on."

He looks at me.

"What?"

"Ma'am, if you don't give me this stuff and get your tail in there and open your email."

"Why didn't you check with your pushy self?

"Um, hello, you sent it from your email account so I couldn't."

"Oh! My bad."

"Yes, your bad now get to going."

I shake my head while handing him the things in my arm. Getting to my desk, I open my laptop and wait for it to power on. Once it does, I login and pull up my email.

"He responded." I say starting to read it.

To: Editor in Chief

Subject: RE: The Forgotten Wife

Wow, is this about you or me? Anyway, I do take responsibility for the part I played but she should have tried harder to talk to me instead of sleeping with some random dude. This is the problem with society now, women are quick to give up instead of fight and now she may be losing a good man. Does cheating have something to do with a woman's self-esteem or something?

Yes, I admit to forgetting her but she never should have cheated. I understand she has needs but she was wrong for the way she handled it. PERIOD.

Sincerely,

Sampson

"What did he say? By the look of your face, it had to be something stupid."

"Read for yourself." I get up from my desk and allow Raul to sit. "If this is what he's like, in real life, I can see why she cheated."

His lips are moving as he reads. He opens his mouth to say something but instead slaps his forehead. "Either this dude thinks he is God's gift to the world or he has to be stuck on stupid. Man, I wish I knew his name because I'd look him up on Facebook."

"I know right but I am glad we don't because this is going to make it even better."

"Please tell me you're about to respond."

"You know I am."

He moves and I take my seat back. I grab the computer and hit the reply button.

To: Sampson

Subject: RE: The Forgotten Wife

You are a piece of work. You say, your wife should have tried harder but I am willing to bet she did. Let me guess, you were too busy being the "good man." How'd that work for you? Maybe you should lose that big ego and actually listen your wife.

Oh and for your information sir, cheating has nothing to do with a woman having low self-esteem. On the contrary, it's all about feeling wanted and appreciated. It is quite obvious your wife needed the attention or she never would have went looking for it. Now, while you may be a good man, you are a terrible husband but it can be fixed. Are you willing?

Signed,

A forgotten wife.

P.S. I plan on printing our email exchanges in a new column of the magazine.

I hit send.

I look up at Raul who is staring at me.

"Get the team in here. We need to revamp the entire middle section of May's issue. This will be the feature."

When he leaves, I walk over to the white board in my office and grab a marker. In big red letters I write the words,

THE FORGOTTEN WIFE!

Todd

Sitting in my office, at Lillie's 2, staring out of the window someone taps on my door.

"Not now!"

The door opens anyway.

"Dang, you still in a foul mood? I thought giving you a few days would have cooled you off by now."

"What do you want Octavia?"

"I'm checking to see if you have come to your senses?"

"As a matter of fact I have. I am willing to give you your last check and time to clean out your locker and vacate the premises."

She laughs while walking towards me, unbuttoning her shirt.

"We both know you don't mean that and I forgive you for choking me."

"Octavia, don't even think about it."

"What am I thinking about?"

"Whatever it is, I want no parts of it. Take your check and leave." I say holding out an envelope.

"Aw, so is this really what you want? Are you firing me because your wife got offended?"

"No, I am firing you because you got complacent and forgot your place."

"My place? Negro, I am nobody's lap dog. You came on to me and not the other way around."

"I did because I thought you could handle the position of being a side piece but clearly I was wrong."

She chuckles. "A side piece? Baby, if anybody is a sidepiece, it's your wife."

"Not anymore. She has been promoted."

"Until your next victim."

"What did you say?"

"You heard me. You're nothing but an egotistical jerk and I hope you get what you deserve because karma is a bitch."

"Well, I'll be sure to let her know you send your regards. Now get out."

"Are you sure this is what you want?"

"I have never been surer of anything."

"Then you leave me no choice."

"What are you talking about?" I ask clasping my hands on the desk.

"I'm going to sue you for sexual harassment."

"Octavia, we both know I did not sexually harass you. If anything, I am the one being sexually harassed. Close your shirt."

"Yea but the courts doesn't. You know with this big *me too* movement, I can say just about anything and they'll go for it."

"Would you really ruin my reputation, marriage and businesses over some meaningless sex?"

"Meaningless sex? You can call it whatever you want but I remember being the one you came home too after working here all night or the one who rubbed your back prior to putting you to sleep and you call it meaningless?"

"Girl, I almost felt something with that little speech." I say pretending to be emotional.

"Forget you Todd. If you think you can mess me over and not feel my wrath, think again. I'll see you in court. Who knows, maybe I'll leak it to the news. Ciao."

She turns to leave.

"Octavia, wait."

She slowly turns with a smile on her face.

"I was hoping it wouldn't have to come to this but, in your words, you leave me no choice."

"Whatever. Do what you want because when it all boils down, it's still on you to prove your innocence. All I have to do is make the accusation."

"You are a pathetic woman."

"Well, I have you to thank for that."

"You may not think so after this." I get up and walk over to the cabinet. "You see, after everything you've pull so far, I knew you would hold true to the threat of blackmail. So, I installed a camera to cover my ass."

She laughs.

"I don't believe you."

I shrug before walking back to my desk. I punch a few keys on the IPad and turn it for her to see.

I press play.

"Yea but the courts doesn't. You know with this whole big me too movement, I can say just about anything and they'll go for it." The video plays.

Her smile quickly fades.

"You son-of-a-bitch."

"Goodbye Octavia."

"Give me my damn check and I will leave."

"Nah, I think we will call it even. Have a nice life boo."

She throws me the middle finger and walks out, passing Roman on the way.

"Everything good boss?"

"No but it will be."

"You finally fired old girl?"

"Look Ramon, I appreciate your concern but I got this."

He laughs. "If you say so." He walks out but then comes back. "Why isn't your wife enough?"

"Excuse you?"

"Why isn't the woman you have at home enough for you?"

"Damn, you act like you got a thing for my wife. Don't you have your own at home?"

"Man, like I told you--"

"I know what you said but that was you and your mistakes. Unlike you, I know how to handle my wife."

He laughs. "This is you handling it?"

"I let Octavia get too close because I wasn't thinking with the right head but it will not happen again."

"What happened to you? When I started here, your wife was all you talked about. Now--"

"Now, she's my business and if you want to keep your fucking job, you will stay out of it. This is my last time telling you."

"Okay." He says throwing his hands up in defense. "But you might be singing a different tune when she finds someone else to do what you won't."

"She already did but it didn't work." I laugh. "She thought having an affair would get my attention and I pretended like it did. I went home and we argued but it did not stop me from going home with Octavia the next night."

"Brother, just when I thought I'd heard it all. I hope you know what you're doing."

"I do. Now, close the door on your way out." I tell him, sitting back at the desk.

Rylee

I was getting ready to turn my car off when I hear Liam's name. I turn up the volume of the radio.

"Prominent Memphis Judge, Liam James will be truly missed by all those who knew him. That he will. Thank you Jerrica. For those of you who just joined us, a family spokesman released a statement on the recent, unexpected passing of Judge Liam James who died from injuries received in a car accident yesterday evening."

I sit there a minute dazed by the news before I turn my car off and make a mad dash into the event space just as this very and I do mean *very*, nice looking man is coming out.

"Hey, are you closing?"

"I am. Can I help you?"

"I had an appointment, thirty minutes ago, with Josie."

"Are you Mrs. Patrick?"

"I am but please call me Rylee."

"Rylee, Josie had an emergency and had to leave. She asked me to wait for you but I didn't think you were coming."

"I am so sorry. I had an emergency at the office but I will not hold you. I'll call Josie in the morning and reschedule."

"No, that will not be necessary. Come on in and I can help you."

"That's okay, I don't want to keep you from your wife."

"There is no wife waiting for me so why don't you come in and allow me to see if I can meet your needs."

I smile at him. "Well okay then."

I feel his eyes on me as I walk pass.

"My name is Maxwell and I believe Josie was supposed to show you around our event space. Is that correct?"

"That's correct."

"Cool. Please follow me and I will show you around. Is there anything specific you want to see this evening?"

"Nothing in particular but everything. I know that sounds weird."

"No, I understand."

"This is my first party, for-"

"For your magazine that has been in business, five years."

"I see you've done your research."

"Of course, I make it a habit to know about everything that happens here."

"Is that right?"

"Of course, especially when it involves a woman as beautiful as you."

"Flattery? I like it."

He smiles.

"We take pride in making sure our clients are pleased." He says looking me up and down. "And I hope you are as equally pleased with what you see."

I feel my jaws heating up as he puts his hand on the small of my back to lead me through the doors.

"How many guests are you expecting?"

"Fifty to seventy-five."

"What about food, are we handling that for you?"

"No, it is being catered and I've already given Josie all of the information. I am planning to have different food stations set up throughout the hall."

"Great. Well, this is the entrance to the main hall where we can have a bar set up, if you plan on having cocktail hour."

"I do."

He leads me through another set of double doors.

"This is the main hall. You can have the tables arranged to your choosing. There is also a stage and we can handle the sound, if you plan on using it."

"Cool."

"Would you like to see the kitchen area, in the back?"

"No, I will not be the one using it so I'll just assume it'll meet the needs of the caterer."

"What about questions?"

"Josie said you all can handle the setup, décor and cleanup. Is that correct?"

"We can." He replies as he continues to walk.

"Awesome. Well, I have seen enough Maxwell. Thank you for taking the time to wait for me."

"It was my pleasure."

"Please have Josie send the final contracts and I will get them signed and sent back with the deposit."

"Or I can bring them if you would like to meet me for lunch or an early dinner."

"Oh, um, I can't. I am married."

"Lucky man." He says.

"He is even though he doesn't realizes it but I'll be sure to tell him you said it."

"Well Mrs. Rylee, whenever you are ready for a taste of a real man, who will appreciate a woman like you, call me." He says kissing the back of my hand. "Until then, I will make sure Josie has the contracts to you by the end of day, tomorrow."

"Thank you again Maxwell. It was great meeting you."

I make it to the car and I have to fan myself. That man was gorgeous, smelled good and can undress you with his eyes. JESUS!

"Good evening Mrs. Rylee, TJ is his room. He has already had dinner and a bath but he isn't quite ready for bed."

"Thank you Maribel."

"You are welcome ma'am. Is there anything else you need before I head home?"

"Yes, there is something I want to discuss with you."

"Yes ma'am, is there something wrong?"

"Nothing is wrong but Todd and I may be separating."

"Oh Mrs. Rylee."

"It will be okay. We, well I am in the process of making final decisions so there is nothing finalized. However, I am sure one of us will be moving out. When that happens, will you be okay taking care of TJ in two separate houses?"

"Yes ma'am."

"Great. It may not come to that but I wanted to make you aware. Once we have the details worked out, I will let you know."

"Thank you Ms. Rylee and I will see you on tomorrow."

Once she leaves, my phone rings with a call from Todd. I put it on speaker.

"What's up Todd?"

"Hey, are you home?"

"I am. Why?"

"I am about to leave the restaurant, headed home."

"What does that have to do with me?"

"Rylee, I know I have no right to ask but can you please wait up for me."

I roll my eyes.

"Todd, we both know you aren't coming home--"

"I am, I promise. I am leaving now."

"Then we shall see."

I hang up and walk into the playroom.

"Mommy!"

"Hey baby, how was your day?"

"Good." He says wrapping his arms around my neck.

"Are you ready for bed?"

He shakes his head no. "Movie."

"Okay." I relent. "Stay here while mommy takes a shower then I'll come back and get you."

"Okay."

I grab the remote to his TV and turn the volume down. I leave his door open before walking into my bedroom to lay my phone on the nightstand.

I get some pajamas and go into the bathroom, leaving the door open in case TJ comes in. I turn on the water, pen my hair up, remove my makeup and undress then step in the shower.

Ten minutes later I get out, dry off, oil my body and get dressed. Turning the light off, I go to get TJ but he is asleep in his chair.

I pick him up and place him in bed. I turn off the light and walk back into my bedroom. I look at my phone and it's been forty-five minutes since Todd called.

Shaking my head, I slide under the covers and grab the remote to catch up on the latest episode of SWAT when I hear a noise up front.

"Todd?"

I mute the TV and throw the cover back. Stepping out of the bedroom door, "Todd--"

Todd

"Hey boss, you headed home?"

"I am but I see the dining room is packed. You sure you don't need me to stay."

"Man, I got this. Go home to your family." Roman says.

I nod at him, grab my bag and head out. Making it to the door, Mateo, my bartender yells my name.

"Todd, I was wondering if I could talk to you about something."

"Can it wait, I really have somewhere to be?"

"Not really. I have another offer for a job."

"You do? Where?"

"There's a new bar opening in Collierville. It's owned by my wife's father and--"

"Say no more. When will you be leaving?"

"Two weeks, maybe three."

"Okay, that's fine and thanks for letting me know. Can we talk more on tomorrow because I would like your help in finding a replacement?"

"Sure thing. I'm sorry to do this to you."

"You don't have to apologize. You are a great worker and even better friend. Your father-in-law would be crazy to have anyone else running his bar."

"Thank you Todd."

I walk out the back door to see Octavia standing next to my truck. I look at my watch and shake my head.

"I don't have time for whatever you are here to do."

"Look, I am sorry about the way I have handled everything."

"Octavia, keep your apology and get off my property."

"Todd, I know I was wrong but the least you can do is give me five minutes when I've given you the last five months of my life."

"The least I can do is not knock you on your ass."

"Why are you being so mean? All I want to do is talk to you."

"Fine. Talk fast?"

"You want to stand here? I don't mind but I know you may not want anyone seeing us."

"Come on but I don't have long."

I unlock the door and she gets in. As soon as I close the door, the phone rings with a call from Rylee but I press ignore.

"What is it? Make it fast because I need to go."

"Oh, now you're in a rush to get home to the wife?"

"Oct--"

"Todd, what happened between us? I thought we were good for each other."

"What we had wasn't a relationship. You knew I had a wife at home."

"Your wife isn't my problem, she's yours and she didn't seem to be a priority when you were spending every night with me."

My phone rings, again, with a call from Rylee but Octavia snatches my phone.

"What are you doing?"

"I'm trying to talk to you." She says dropping the phone on the floor. "I know I messed up but can't we fix this some kind of way"

She leans over and kisses me.

"Please." She coos. "Can't we fix this?"

"No."

"Come on Todd, one last time."

Her hand slides down between my legs. For a moment, I lay my head back on the seat.

"You know you miss the feel of my mouth."

When I feel her unzipping my pants, I don't stop her.

"Tell me you want this?"

I don't say anything and for the next ten minutes, she pleases me in the truck, in the parking lot of my restaurant.

When she is done, she kisses me on the lips. I push her away and fix my pants.

"Come home with me."

"I can't."

"Damn it Todd. What about my feelings?"

"Get out."

"Are you serious? After everything I have done for you?" She cries.

"Baby, the only things you are good at is handling my hard cock and a dinner service but you aren't the only one capable of those responsibilities. Next time, stay in your place."

She wipes her face. "Can I at least get my last check? I need the money."

"Fine but do not come here again."

I get my bag from the back seat and give her the check.

"I mean it Octavia. Do not come here again."

She opens the door and stops. "Can I ask you a question?"

"Yes and then you'll have to get out."

"What if you didn't have a wife?"

"What?"

"If you didn't have a wife, could you love me?"

"Why would you ask me that?"

"It was just a question. Goodbye Todd."

When she gets out, I fix my clothes and pull off.

I turn down the street to see police lights in front of my house. I put the truck in park and jump out.

"Whoa sir, you cannot go in there." A police officer says.

"This is my house."

"You still cannot go in."

"Where is my wife and son?"

"Stay here."

He walks over to another man who points to me. They begin walking towards me.

"Sir, my name is Detective Hunter Collins, what is your name?"

"Todd Patrick. Is my wife and son alright?"

"We've been trying to reach you Mr. Patrick." He says.

"Where is my wife and son?"

"Sir, I am sorry to have to tell you this but your wife was the victim of an attack tonight."

"What? Where is she?"

"She has been transported to Regional One."

"Where is my son? Was he hurt?"

"No. He's with a member of social services."

"Was it a home invasion or something?"

"We are not sure but we are investigating. Do you know if your wife had any enemies?"

"Enemies? No, of course not."

"What about you?"

I instantly think of Octavia but I say no.

"Detective, can you at least tell me if my wife is alive?"

"The doctors will have to discuss that with you, at the hospital." He says. "Now, I need to ask you some more questions."

"Where is my son?"

He motions for an officer who walks over holding TJ and he is crying.

"Daddy." He says reaching out his arms.

"I'm here."

"Mommy," he cries burying his head into my shoulder.

"I know, we will find mommy. Detective can I please take my son to his nanny? He's been through enough already."

"For now but I will need to get him in front of a detective who specializes in speaking with children who have seen trauma."

"Wait, are you saying--"

"We don't know what he saw, hence the reason we need him to speak to a detective."

I squeeze him tighter as I begin to cry.

"Who would do this to her?"

"We don't know but we were hoping you did."

"Detective, I will answer any questions you have but first I need to get to my wife."

I walk back to my truck and when I try to put TJ in his seat, he starts to scream. It takes me over five minutes to get him calm.

When I finally get into the driver's seat, I reach over and grab my phone from the floor, realizing Octavia turned it off. When I power it on, I have five voicemails. I ignore them and call Maribel. I try to explain a little of what's going on before letting her know I am headed to her house.

"Sir, can I help you?"

"I was told my wife was bought here by ambulance. Her name is Rylee, R-Y-L-E-E Patrick."

She taps on the computer.

"She is still being triaged by the doctors. Go through the double doors and to the end of the hall. There is button on the wall, push it and the nurses there can assist you."

I nervously wait over thirty minutes until a nurse calls my name. I follow her back to the trauma bay.

"Dr. Ware, this is Mr. Patrick." She says.

"Doctor, how is my wife?"

"She is stable but she suffered lacerations to her face and neck, some broken ribs on both sides as well as a broken ankle. We will need to repair her ankle with surgery."

"Can I see her?"

"Yes but she is sedated."

I go into her room and my heart drops at the sight of her. Her face is swollen and covered in cuts.

"Oh my God, who would do this to you?" I ask rubbing her face.

She opens her eyes.

"Rylee baby, I am right here."

"Where were you?" She whispers before the machines start to beep.

The nurses run in.

"Sir, we're going to have to ask you to step out."

"What's happening?"

"Sir, please!"

After a few minutes of waiting, Dr. Ware comes out.

"Doctor, what happened?"

"She has what is called a traumatic pneumothorax. It means her right lung collapsed from being punctured by the broken ribs. We've had to insert a chest tube to help her breathe and she will need immediate surgery. A nurse will keep you updated."

I begin to pace when my phone rings with a call from an unknown number. I press decline but a few seconds later, it rings again.

"Yeah, hello."

"Todd-" the phone is breaking up.

"Octavia?"

There is a lot of noise.

"Todd, I'm sorry."

"Octavia, I cannot hear you."

"I didn't mean—"

"You didn't mean what?"

She is saying something but I can't make it out.

"If I find out you had anything to do with attacking my wife, I'll kill you."

I release the call and turn to find Detective Collins standing there.

"Sir, would you like to tell me what's going on, here or down at the station."

Detective Hunter Collins

"Am I under arrest?"

"Mr. Patrick, if you were under arrest, I would have you in an interrogation room instead of this employee lounge. This is simply us having a conversation. Do you know what happened to your wife?"

"No."

"Where were you tonight?"

"At my restaurant." I tell him.

"Do you have someone who can corroborate your statement?"

"Yes, my staff. Look detective, I have watched enough crime shows to know the spouse is the first suspect but I did not do this."

"Then who did?" He asks. "And do not lie to me because I heard your conversation and you know more than you're saying."

"I--, I had an affair."

He sits back in the chair.

"Go on."

"My wife found out about it and I broke it off."

"Do you think the woman you were having an affair with did this?"

"Not unless she hired somebody."

"How can you be sure?"

"We were together tonight." I whisper.

"I'm sorry, I didn't hear you."

"We were together tonight."

"So, you were laying up with another woman while your wife was getting the crap beat out of her?"

"NO! It is not what you think. I didn't sleep with her."

"You just said you were with the woman you're having an affair with. Isn't that what you JUST said?"

"We didn't have sex, she gave me oral in the truck."

"Does she have the capability to pay somebody to do this?"

"I guess."

"Look, you and these nonchalant answers are starting to piss me off. Man, I saw the condition of your wife and whoever did this to her, it was personal. So cut the crap before I haul your ass down to the station!"

"Sir, I don't know if Octavia did this for sure but I don't put it pass her because she was angry about me ending thing. I also think she was following Rylee because there was a note left on her car, a few Sundays ago."

"What did the note say?"

"Something about her needing to pray I stay home and out of her bed."

"Do you still have the note?"

"No, I threw it out."

"And you didn't think to report this?"

"I contacted my lawyer to get a restraining order but I didn't think she would go to this extreme."

"Was that before or after you had sex with her again?"

"I know how this looks but I didn't mean for things to go this far."

"What is Octavia's last name?"

"Wright."

"When did this affair start?"

"About five months ago?"

"Where did you meet her?"

"At my restaurant, she was my Sous Chef."

He stops writing and looks at me.

"Detective, I never meant for my wife to be hurt."

"Your wife was hurt the moment you started the affair. Sit tight for me."

"Do you know how much longer this is going to take, I need to check on my wife."

"As long as it needs to."

He walks out and I hit the table with my fists. My phone vibrates and I jump. I hurriedly get it out of my pocket to see a text from an unknown number.

I open it to find a picture of Octavia, naked.

Me: Stop freaking texting me.

A few seconds later, she replies.

HER: Or what?

ME: Just leave me alone.

HER: How's the wife?

Then she sends the laughing emoji.

A few minutes later, Detective Collins comes back.

"Is this Octavia Wright?" He asks showing me a picture on his phone.

"Yea and she just text me."

I show him the phone.

"It looks like you have a real live one on your hands. You're free to go but I need to warn you not to leave town."

Rylee

I open my eyes to see Todd asleep with his hand wrapped around mine. I move it away, causing him to wake up.

"Baby--"

"Don't." I whisper, grimacing in pain. "Where is TJ?"

"He's with Maribel."

"How long have I been here?"

"Two days. Let me get the doctor." He says, starting to get up.

"Where were you?"

He drops his head and sits back in the chair.

"I have no excuse for not being there, I'm sorry."

I close my eyes as the tears sting the side of my face.

"You said you were coming."

"Rylee, I am sorry. I should have been there but what's to say this wouldn't have still happened?"

"Get out."

The door opens and a man walks in. Todd stands to greet him.

"Mrs. Patrick, my name is Detective Collins, how are you this morning?"

"In pain."

He nods.

"Is now a good time to answer some questions?"

I nod my head.

"Can you tell me what happened the other night at your house?"

I close my eyes to remember. "It hadn't been long since I'd arrived home. I took a shower before putting TJ to bed." I pause from the pain. "I had just gotten in bed when I heard a noise. I thought it was Todd," I stop again. "I thought it was Todd because he said he was on the way so I got up." I pause again. "When I stepped out the bedroom, someone hit me."

"Did you see who your attacker was?"

"I wasn't able to see his face but I know it was a man. He chased me back into the bedroom but I was able to get to my phone. Todd was the last person who called so I tried to call him, for help but--" I stop when I feel the tears. "I tried calling him but he didn't answer."

"Do you have any idea how he got in?"

"No but I didn't hear a door open."

"Is there an alarm?"

"No." Todd says. "We never needed one."

"He knew me." I blurt.

"Who?" Collins asks.

"He called me by name. After he was done, he called my name." I groan in pain as the tears slide from my eyes.

"Do you remember what he said?"

"I didn't mean for this to happen Rylee but she didn't leave me a choice."

"She? Did he say who she was?"

"No but I am pretty sure I know who did this."

"Who?"

"Todd's girlfriend."

"Octavia?" Collins questions. "Why do you suspect her?"

"Nobody else has a reason to want me out of the picture. Unless my husband does."

"Wait, just hold on!" Todd screams. "I would never want this for you. I love you Rylee."

"Yea, well I don't believe it."

"Do you honestly think I would have you attacked at our house, in front of our son?"

I don't say anything.

"Rylee, please say you don't believe I would do this. You know me."

"No Todd, I used to know you."

"Mrs. Patrick, I will do everything I can to find out who did this to you. In the meantime, I am going to put a guard outside your door."

"Thank you detective but can you also do one more thing?"

"Sure."

"Get my husband out of here."

It's been a week since I was attacked. I was finally released from the hospital, a couple of days ago and it has been a struggle getting around with broken ribs and ankle.

"Mrs. Riley, someone is here to see you." Maribel whispers.

I look up to see Raul. "Thank you Maribel. Okay Rae, I'm going to let you go and I'll see you when you get back. I love you too."

I hang up and lay the phone on the arm of the couch.

"Hey, how are you feeling?" Raul asks when I lay the phone down.

"Much better. How are things at the office?"

"We have things under control. You let us handle that while you get better."

"You know that's hard for me to do. Is May's issue complete?"

"Yes, I have the mock up for you."

"Great. Did Maxwell Planning ever send the contracts for the party?"

He rolls his eyes. "Are you even supposed to be working?"

"Boy, if you don't give me those contracts. Work doesn't stop for sickness."

He laughs. "Here."

"Thank you. Now, did Sampson respond to the last email?"

"Yep."

"And?"

"See for yourself." He says, handing me his tablet.

To: Forgotten Wife

Subject: RE: The Forgotten Wife

You seem to know an awful lot about cheating. Let me guess, you've cheated previously. Figures. But to answer your question, yes my wife tried to talk to me but I was too busy taking care of her and our home. Forgive me for wanting to give her a great lifestyle, in which she thanks me by cheating. Yet here I am, writing a magazine for help to fix my marriage. Doesn't that count for something? Look, I realize my fault in all of this but I am willing to change and even forgive her. Are you willing to help or not because I don't want to lose my family?"

Sincerely,

Sampson

P.S. I don't mind you printing this because maybe it'll stop other wives from cheating on good men who make mistakes.

"Wow, this dude is a real piece of crap."

"At least he agreed to let us use the emails." Raul says.

"Yes, that is definitely a win but did you notice he changed my name from editor-in-chief to forgotten wife?"

"Yes. I think it's to mock you."

I laugh. "Have you all had a chance to come up with something for marketing?"

"Are you going to respond?"

"Of course I am, after you show me what you have."

"Alright Ms. Thang." He pulls some boards from his bag. "Here is what I was thinking. A black background with the words, The Forgotten Wife, in red block letters and a catchy slogan. I also have it in white and blue."

"I like the concept but I think adding a woman in the background, looking away with a veil over her face will make it pop."

"Cool." He says making notes. "Regarding the slogan, I jotted down a few from the ladies in the office and social media."

"Let me hear them."

"The forgotten wife who wasn't forgotten."

"Hmm, what else?"

"Forget about me now, remember me later."

"I like that. What else?"

"Forgotten by the one who vowed to remember. The forgotten wife but she hasn't forgotten. The forgotten wife whom will always be remembered or forgotten now, remembered later."

"You got anymore?"

"The forgotten wife who never forgot or forget me till I'm gone."

"Wow, all of those are pretty good. Which ones stick out to you?"

"I am leaning towards, forgotten by the one who vowed to remember."

"Me too but let me sleep on it and get back with you."

"Okay. Is there anything else you need me to do?"

"Can you get my laptop out of my office?"

"Sure."

When he comes back, he gives me the mockup of May's magazine along with the slogans he just read off and the contract for the party.

After he leaves, I open my computer to respond to the email.

To: Sampson

Subject: RE: The Forgotten Wife

Dear Sampson,

Just when I think I can't dislike you even more, your email comes in. I apologize for getting my personal feelings involved but I do speak from experience. However, this is not about me. Question though. What is the purpose of working to create a great life, for your family, to only have to split it in the divorce? Your wife would probably agree, she'd rather have her husband at home, making love to her more than a new pair of shoes any night of the week.

Do not misunderstand me because I know the value of working hard but I am willing to bet your wife works too. Did she forget you? There has to be balance and it comes from both of you being on the same page. Sure, your wife made a mistake and I will not put the blame entirely on you but you have fault too.

To answer your question as to what you do now. Work on saving your marriage by making her a priority, coming home to eat those meals (if she still cooks for you) and showing her you love and appreciate her; physically and not just financially. Sir, it's not rocket science.

Good luck.

Signed,

A forgotten wife.

Todd

I walk into the house and drop my bag onto the kitchen counter. I grab a bottle of water from the refrigerator and turn out the light.

Walking into the living room, I see Rylee's computer on the coffee table.

I sit in front of it and rub my hand over the mouse pad. It comes up to her email.

"The Forgotten Wife," I mouthed while scrolling to the beginning of the thread. "Wow."

I close the laptop and when I get up, I jump at the sight of Rylee.

"Were you on my computer?" She asks.

"Have I made you feel like a forgotten wife?"

"What do you think?"

"Rylee, I don't want to argue with you tonight."

"Then don't."

"Why are you up? Tell me what you need and I'll get it for you."

"I need my husband but seeing you aren't available, I'll take some water and a pain pill."

I get what she needs and hand it to her.

"Goodnight."

"Rylee, wait."

"What Todd?"

"I am so sorry for everything that has happened because of me."

"Thanks."

"Will you at least talk to me?"

"Now you want to talk, at 3:30 in the morning? Don't you think it's too late for that?"

"Well, we are both up."

"No, it's too late as in, I no longer have anything to say."

"Baby it's not too late. We can fix this."

"Fix what exactly because from the looks of your life, everything is good?"

"Everything is not good. I am hurting, just like you."

"You sure because as I recall it, I was the one beaten while our son lay crying in his room from hearing the screams of his mom. Are you sure because it hurts when I take a deep breath, what about you? Are you absolutely sure because it hurts for me to put full weight on my ankle, what about you?"

"Rylee, you know what I mean."

"No, I hear what you are saying. Todd, we both know this was Octavia. A woman scorn because my husband has community penis. Hell, what's to say she won't try again?"

"We don't even know if it was Octavia. For all we know, it was the dude you slept with."

She steps back and looks at me shocked. "I cannot believe you're covering for her? I could have died and you're covering for your bitch. No boo, it couldn't have been the dude I was sleeping with because he's dead."

My eyes grow wide with shock.

"Yeah," she continues, "so any other suggestions?"

"I did not mean to seem like I was covering for her. I was only saying we don't know for sure who did this."

"If it wasn't her then it had to be you."

I let out a breath.

"No denial," she taunts. "Interesting."

"You know I'd never do anything like that."

"No, I don't actually."

I let out a long breath. "Rylee, I am trying."

"What are you trying to do exactly?"

"I am trying to be here for you."

"Oh," she laughs. "You're trying to be here and yet it's after three and you're just getting home."

"I am trying."

"Todd, do you know how hard it is to be in this house? I am afraid to sleep, your son will not sleep in his room because he is having nightmares and neither will he let me out of his sight. If it weren't for Maribel, I wouldn't get a break but you're trying. Okay."

"I'm sorry for not being here but I don't know what to do for you. It's hard to face you."

"It's hard to face me? HOW DO YOU THINK I FEEL? I am the one who is faced with scars that have not healed. I am the one faced with moments of unimaginable pain and I am the one who was faced with my blood, stained in the carpet of our bedroom floor. Dude, facing me should not be hard unless you're guilty of something."

"I am not guilty of anything, I just didn't know." I tell her as TJ cries out for her.

"You wouldn't know because you are never here."

"Please Rylee. I am here now."

"It's too late."

"But you said you've give us thirty days."

"Screw your thirty days."

The next morning, I jump up from the couch, when I hear the beeping of a truck backing into the driveway.

"What's going on?" I ask Rylee who is coming down the hall.

She doesn't answer and instead goes over to open the door.

"Good morning, are you Rylee Patrick?"

"I am."

"Ma'am, I am Arthur Clemmons with Clemmons Moving and I have an order to get you moved."

"That will be correct. Come in and I will show you where to begin. I have marked everything that's going with me. There is all of the furniture from my son's room, some things in the office as well as the master bedroom and kitchen." Rylee says. "You shouldn't have a problem but if you have a question, I'll be around."

"Is this the address where your things are to be delivered?" He asks showing her his phone.

"Yep, that's it."

"Thank you ma'am. We will get started."

"Rylee, what is going on?" I ask her again.

"What does it look like Todd? TJ and I are moving out."

"Moving out? Where?"

Just then there is a knock on the open door.

"Is this a bad time?" Detective Collins asks walking in.

"Detective, what can we do for you?" I ask him.

"Can we sit?" He requests.

"Sure."

"Mrs. Patrick, we found the man we believe was responsible for attacking you. Do either of you recognize him?" He says showing a picture.

"No, who is he?" Rylee ask.

"His name is Grant Nelson."

"Why would he attack me?"

"We don't know."

"What do you mean, you don't know. You got him in custody, ask him." Rylee demands.

"He's not in custody. When I said, we found him, I meant his body."

"Then how do you know it was him?" I inquire.

"He left a video recording. Have either of you heard of the movie Strangers on a Train?"

"The old movie where two people conspire to murder someone for the other person?" Rylee asks with me looking at her.

"Yes." Detective Collins says. "Apparently Mr. Nelson and this mystery person talked about trading murders, over eight years ago. He said in the video, he only went along with it because he assumed it was a joke. Until his wife's body was found in an alley."

"Why didn't he tell someone?"

"Well, here's where it gets tricky. Grant's wife, Gina Nelson was murdered a year ago so he didn't think her death had anything to do with this arrangement. The police listed is as a robbery until a package showed up at his office with a note calling in the favor."

"What else will it take for you all to believe this is Octavia?" Rylee says.

"We've been trying to locate Ms. Wright. Have either of you had any recent contact with her?"

I look at Rylee. "Um, not since the night my wife was attacked."

"If you hear from her, let me know immediately." Collins says standing. "As I said beforehand, I will find out who did this to you Mrs. Patrick. In the meantime, if you need anything don't hesitate to call."

I walk Detective Collins out. When I come back, Rylee is pacing.

"You were with her the night I was attacked?"

"Rylee, it wasn't like that. She showed up at the restaurant when I was leaving."

"So, she could have held you up knowing someone was coming here to attack me?"

I can't say anything.

"Did you have sex with her?"

"Yes but it was just oral."

She turns to walk away.

"Rylee, it was just oral sex."

"Yea, well it is also just your marriage."

Rylee

THREE WEEKS LATER

"Rylee, there is a Maxwell Carpenter to see you." Natalie buzzes.

"Maxwell Carpenter?" I say to myself before pressing the intercom button. "Send him in."

I stand and walk to the front of my desk as the door opens.

"Mr. Carpenter, what do I owe this visit?" I ask extending my hand.

"I was in the neighborhood and decided to stop in--are you okay?" He asks when he sees the boot on my leg.

"This old thing." I laugh. "Yes, I will be fine. I just came out of a cast and have to wear this thing for another few weeks."

He looks like he wants to ask more but he doesn't.

"Is something wrong?"

"Oh no and I apologize for dropping by without an appointment but I wanted to make sure everything was okay because we haven't received the contract back for your party. Have you changed your mind?"

"Shit, the contract."

He laughs.

"I apologize for my language and not getting back to you. I've had so much going on."

I go behind my desk and begin moving paper around. "It's here somewhere."

"I didn't come to rush you into signing. I wanted to make sure there was nothing we did to make you change your mind about utilizing our services."

"I see." I smile. "So you make personal visits to sway your customers?"

His face turns red.

"I'm kidding. No, I have plans to utilize your services. To prove it, I will find, sign and get the contracts back to you by tomorrow."

"Great."

He stands there.

"Is there something else?"

He doesn't get to answer because Todd comes bursting in with Natalie behind him.

"You had me served at my restaurant!"

"Rylee, I tried to stop him."

"Thank you Natalie, will you show Mr. Carpenter out for me?" I turn back to Maxwell. "I am sorry about this. I will get those contracts signed and sent to you."

"No problem. I will be in touch."

I walk them to the door and close it.

"What the hell were you thinking?" Todd yells before I even turn around.

"First, you need to lower your voice."

"Why? You don't want me to embarrass you, the way you embarrassed me?"

"You got some nerve."

"Me? You had divorce papers served at my freaking business and in front of my staff. Do you know how that made me look?"

"Oh, now we care about how we make each other look? Spare me the dramatics Todd. If you cared about me, we wouldn't be here now."

"No, we are here because you know nothing about forgiveness. I made a mistake and now you want to throw away what we've built."

I start to laugh. "Wait, are you serious right now?"

"I'm glad you find this funny."

"No boo, I find you funny. You got the audacity to stand here talking about forgiveness. Mane bye. Sign the papers and let me get on with my life. Who knows, maybe you and Octavia can get married in the prison chapel."

"Rylee, I know I hurt you and I'm sorry but don't throw away what we have. It's only been two weeks, can we at least try to work this out?"

"Baby, the only thing we have to work out is the details of this divorce. And for the record, it's been three weeks but whose counting."

"How did you even have the papers drawn up this fast?"

"Money has the power to get anything done. Now, if you'll excuse me I have work to do."

"This isn't fair."

"Haven't you heard, life isn't fair?"

"Rylee--"

"Goodbye Todd."

"I will not let you divorce me." He says throwing the envelope down on the desk and storming out.

Ten minutes later, Natalie buzzes.

"Not now Natalie."

"Rylee, Maribel is on line one."

I quickly snatch the handle of the phone.

"Maribel is--oh my God, where are you? I'm on the way."

Todd

Walking out of Rylee's office, my phone rings from an unknown number. I press ignore while getting into the truck and pushing the start button.

My phone rings again.

I press the button on the steering wheel.

"Yea."

"Having fun yet?" A disguised voice asks.

"Hello."

"Don't act like you didn't hear me."

"Who is this?"

"I asked if you were enjoying the game."

"Look, I am not in the mood for this!"

"I suggest you buckle up because we are just getting started."

The call hangs up just as Rylee comes limping out of the building looking frantic. I get out the truck.

"What's wrong?"

"It's TJ, he's missing."

"Maribel, what happened?" Rylee asks, rushing towards her.

"Mrs. Rylee, I am so sorry."

"Maribel, just tell us what happened."

She is upset and crying so her Spanish accent is very heavy.

"TJ was playing with another little boy, on the slide. I turned around to get his cup and when I looked back he was gone."

"Oh my God!" Rylee cries as Detective Collins walks up.

"Detective Collins, please tell me you have found my son." I say.

He shakes his head as Rylee lets out a scream.

I grab her.

"How long has he been gone?"

"For about an hour."

"Mr. Todd, I only looked away for a second. I am so sorry, I didn't mean for this to happen."

Just then someone calls Detective Collins through his radio.

"Collins, we got something on the East end of the park."

"I'll be right there. Stay here until you hear from me." He says.

I walk Rylee over to a bench.

"Todd, they have to find my baby."

Ten minutes later, Detective Collins' car pulls in. Rylee and I stand up as he comes over to us.

"We found TJ."

"Where is he?"

"The hospital."

Fifteen minutes later we rush into LeBonheur Children's Hospital.

The nurse takes us into an examination room where TJ is laying on the bed.

"Mommy," he says sounding groggy.

"Hey baby. Mommy is so happy to see you."

"Are you the parents?" A doctor questions when he walks in.

"Why can't he stay awake?"

"We are trying to figure that out. Is he currently on any medication?"

I look at Rylee.

"No, just a daily vitamin." She answers.

"Has he hit his head recently or suffered a concussion?"

"No, why are you asking these kinds of questions? Did something happen to him?"

"Although we do not believe your son has been physically hurt, he may have been given something to make him drowsy. We don't know what so I have to ask these questions to ensure nothing counteracts what is already in his system. The nurse has drawn blood and while we wait on the results, we will allow him to sleep it off. I will be back once I know more."

When he leaves, Rylee and I turn to Detective Collins.

"Do you know who did this?" I ask.

"We both know who did this!" Rylee rages. "This is all your fault. Get out!"

"I will leave but only to talk to Detective Collins and allow you to calm down but I will be back."

Walking out of the room, my phone vibrates. I pull it out of my pocket to two text messages from an unknown number. I open the first text and it is a picture of TJ sleeping on a park bench. I scroll to the next.

TEXT: Game on sir.

"Detective, you need to see this."

Rylee

The next afternoon, we are finally being released to go home. All of TJ's test came back clear and the doctor confirms he was given some kind of sleep aid.

He spoke to the same lady, from the police department, who specializes in questioning children but all he remembers is someone grabbing him from the slide and giving him a Popsicle.

"Hey," Todd says coming into the room.

"Daddy," he exclaims before giving me a hug.

"Hey little man, how are you feeling?"

"Good. I'm going home with mommy."

"I know." I say rubbing his head.

"Why are you here?" I ask him.

"I came to take you and TJ home."

"No thank you."

"Look Rylee, I know you are upset but I am here to help."

"I think you've done enough."

"Why are you blaming me for this?"

"Are you serious? TJ, go and play over there while mommy talks to daddy."

I wait until he walks away.

"All of this is because you cannot keep your penis in your pants. You bought this into our lives. Not me, YOU!" She says through clenched teeth.

"Look, I get that you are upset but now is not the time for you to move out. You and TJ need to be at home."

"Oh so you can protect us. Ha! That's a joke. You couldn't protect us before, what makes you think you can now."

"I am going to take some time off until Detective Collins and his team figure this out."

"What's to figure out? We both know this is Octavia. Find her and this will stop."

"We don't know that."

A nurse comes in with the discharge paperwork and a wagon for TJ to ride downstairs. Once I am done loading our things, I turn back to Todd.

"Stay away from us."

TJ and I have been staying in our new condo for almost three weeks. It took some getting used to but it is our new normal now and it has security which has been the biggest plus.

I have been working from home, trying to get everything finalized for the new blog and feature for The Forgotten Wife.

Finishing up lunch, my cell phone rings with a call from Raul.

"Rylee, oh my God, have you seen the email?"

"Hello to you too."

"Sorry, hey, have you seen the email?"

"No, what happened?" I inquire. "It must be good because--"

"Rylee, stop what you are doing and read it NOW!" He exclaims. "NOW please and call me back."

Before I can respond, he hangs up.

I walk into the living room with TJ's sandwich, chips and juice. I sit it on the table in front of him and grab my laptop.

To: Forgotten Wife

Subject: RE: The Forgotten Wife

I am tired of playing this game. Surprise, there is no Sampson. I wrote this email, not knowing if you would take the bait but you did. While I thank you for your advice, it is too late because my husband left me. As a matter of fact, it has been about eight years since he walked out on me ... and married YOU!

And now, you're me. Funny how life is. I know you are probably trying to figure out why I would come after you and not Todd but it'll all make sense soon. So, hold tight because the game is just beginning. Oh, the attack wasn't meant to kill you but it did get you to move.

Nice condo, by the way.

Until next time,

The real forgotten wife

My hand flies to my mouth and the ringing of my phone causes me to jump.

"Rae," I cry into the phone.

"Rylee, what's wrong? Is it TJ?"

I can't say anything.

"Rylee, talk to me."

"I know who attacked me." I say walking away from TJ.

"Who?"

"Todd's first wife. Let me call you back."

I release the call without giving her a chance to say anything else. Immediately dialing Detective Collins' number, I let him know I need to see him. After giving him my new address, I hang up and dial Todd's number.

"Hey, I was just about to call you." He says.

"Why didn't you tell me you were married previously?"

"What?"

"Todd, cut the BS. Were you married prior to me?"

He sighs.

"It was a long time ago. How did you find out?"

"The source."

"What do you mean?"

"What in the hell do you think I mean. She contacted me."

"Who?"

"Did you not just hear me or are you playing stupid?"

"Rylee, I don't know what you mean?"

"Your fucking ex-wife, is what I mean. She contacted me."

"I'm on my way to you."

"Don't bother."

"Rylee, I know you are upset but there are some things you need to know. I'm coming over!"

He hangs up on me.

I begin to pace before I sit to read the email again. You know, just to make sure it said what it said.

I send Raul a text.

ME: Has anyone else seen this email?

RAUL: Just me. Are you okay? Who is this woman?

ME: I don't know but I am going to find out. In the meantime, I do not want anyone else to see it. To answer your question, I am not okay.

RAUL: What about the feature?

ME: Continue to work on it. I don't want anyone to know something is wrong.

RAUL: Is there something wrong?

ME: Obviously but I don't know what.

RAUL: Are you going to respond?

ME: I don't know yet.

RAUL: Be careful Rylee.

ME: I will.

I hit send as the landline phone rings from security. I go to answer it.

"Mrs. Patrick, you have a visitor."

"Who is it?"

"Raegan Haywood." He says as I hear someone else talking in the back. "And a Detective Collins. And Todd Patrick."

"Send them up."

Todd

"Rylee, what is going on?" Raegan asks rushing by me.

"Ask Todd." She says causing all them to turn to me. "TJ baby, come and let mommy put a movie on for you."

Rylee doesn't give him a chance to even speak to me.

I walk back into the living and immediately begin talking. "I got an email from someone claiming to be Todd's wife. She asserts to being behind the attack. The email said, it wasn't to kill me but to get me to move. She even mentioned about this condo being nice."

"Todd, who is this?" Rae asks.

I rub my head.

"TALK!" Rylee yells.

We all sit.

"I have been married before, twice."

"Wow." Rylee says. "Who are you because apparently I don't know who the hell I am married too."

"Rylee, I am sorry--"

"Man, screw your apology because it doesn't do crap for me and our son when our lives are on the line."

"Whoa, calm down." Collins says. "Todd, go on."

"My second wife's name was Laylah. I met her when she would come to Memphis on business. I was still married to my first wife and—"

"So you've always been a cheater?" Rylee inserts.

I look at her and she rolls her eyes.

"Anyway. Laylah and I had an affair for over a year. She decided to leave her husband and was pressuring me to finalize my divorce. When I wasn't moving as fast as she wanted, she moved back to South Carolina. I found out, months later, she was pregnant. To make a long story short--"

"Oh no, we got time." Raegan says.

"I finalized my divorce and moved to South Carolina. Laylah and I got married at the courthouse and everything was great until it wasn't. Marrying her turned out to be the worst mistake of my life."

"Why?" Collins asks.

"For starters, she had trust issues with men that stemmed from an incident when she was in college."

"What kind of incident?"

"When she was nineteen, she was gang raped by a group of boys at a party. Ever since then, she was never the same. In and out of hospitals and on all kinds of drugs. Her family kept this from me because she made them believe she was better."

"What happened to the baby?" Rylee says.

"She died."

"How?"

I look down at my hands.

"Uh hello." She says snapping her fingers. "What happened to the baby?"

"Laylah was attacked, in our home, the morning of her baby shower. She and the baby died."

"Attacked by who?"

I shrug.

"Was it you?" Raegan asks.

"No, I wasn't even in town. Her family and even the police suspected me but I was here, for the Memorial Day weekend. Laylah and I wasn't on the best of terms, by then."

"You're lying." Rylee angrily yells. "What man isn't there for his wife's baby shower?"

"Me. I wasn't there because she tried to kill me."

Rylee laughs. "Is this a badly written horror movie? Next you're going to say, she isn't really dead."

"She is." I confirm.

"Todd, why did Laylah try to kill you?" Collins ask.

"She thought I was cheating."

"Were you?"

"No but she was convinced because somebody was sending her messages and leaving notes on her car. She was so paranoid. I guess it got to be too much because one night I woke up to our bedroom being on fire."

Rylee laughs. "Negro, are you telling me she pulled a burning bed on you? This has got to be the funniest stuff I have heard in a long time."

She gets up and begin pacing.

"Let me get this straight." Rae says. "Your wife and child is murdered, you are a suspect but it is never proven and you pack up and move back to Memphis like she never existed."

"I didn't have a reason to stay there."

"And you didn't think my sister deserved to know this?" Raegan screams.

"It was part of my past. I haven't heard from or seen any of Laylah's family since the night of her funeral. I didn't have a reason too."

"Someone seems to think otherwise."

Rylee

The air gets caught in my throat and I begin coughing.

"Rylee, are you okay? Breathe." Raegan demands, patting me on the back.

"Wa-wa-water," I get out.

Todd jumps up and runs into the kitchen, returning with a bottle of water. After a few sips, I regain my composure and wipe the tears that are falling.

I turn to Todd. "If Laylah is really dead, who is stalking me?"

"I don't know."

"You don't know?" I repeat. "Let me get away from you before I knock your ass out."

"Todd, can you think of anyone else who can be doing this?" Detective Collins ask. "It has to be someone who knew the intricate details of your relationship with Laylah."

"Did you see the body?" Raegan asks.

"No, the coroner advised against it."

"That's bullshit. You were her husband, you could have seen her if you wanted too. You're lying." I scream.

"I'm telling the truth."

"So, there is a possibility she's not dead?"

"Why would she fake her own death?"

"She was your wife so you tell us?" Rae says.

"Todd, what is Laylah's date of birth?" Collins request.

"January twelfth, 1976."

Detective Collins walks out into the hall.

"Rylee--"

"No Todd, you cannot explain your way out of this. Your dead psycho ex-wife or someone pretending to be her is trying to kill me. Why?"

"I wish I could answer that but I don't know why any of this is happening. Rylee, you have to know it was never my intent to hurt you."

"Spare me." I tell him. "Since you don't know what's going on, I'll find out."

"What do you mean?"

"I'm going to respond to the email."

"No Rylee," Raegan states. "You cannot do that."

"Who is going to stop me?"

I walk over to my computer but Detective Collins walks in.

"I have my partner pulling the information on Laylah Patrick. Once I have more, I'll be in touch."

When he leaves, I turn back to Raegan and Todd looking at me. I push pass them to the computer.

"Rylee, you cannot respond. You don't know who it is." Rae says.

"That's even more reason too."

To: ~~Sampson~~ Dead Ex-Wife

Subject: RE: The Forgotten Wife

Unless God has added Wi-Fi to the afterlife, you are not Todd's ex-wife so cut the bullshit! You have gone through all this trouble of pretending to be a husband who loves his wife but we know this isn't the case. Now you're a dead ex-wife, which isn't true either. So, what is it? Did my husband sleep with you, promising you the world and didn't deliver? Did he make you assurances, while pillow talking after sex and broke your heart? What?

Tell me, killer, why is this my fault? Hell, if this is about Todd, beat his ass and leave me alone. However, if you insist on coming after me, show yourself and stop hiding behind a computer because I will no longer live in fear of you. Whoever in the hell you are, if you want to play, let's play!

Signed,

Still a forgotten wife.

Detective Hunter Collins

"Good afternoon, are you Kaylah Gilmore?"

"I am, who's asking?"

"My name is Detective Hunter Collins with the Memphis Police Department. Do you mind if I come in and speak with you?"

"Memphis? What are you doing in South Carolina?"

"I wanted to ask some questions about your sister Laylah."

"Laylah?"

"Yes ma'am."

"Come in." She says stepping back to let me through the door. "Can I get you something to drink?"

"No thank you."

"Okay, so what can I do for you detective?"

"We have reason to believe someone pretending to be your sister is stalking Todd and his wife. Or, are my assumptions right and your sister isn't dead."

She laughs. "You know what they say about assumptions, detective."

"Yes but tell me I am wrong."

"Let's say, hypothetically, my sister is alive. What makes you think she is the one who doing whatever it is, to Todd?"

"This email."

I hand her a copy of it.

"Wow." She says after reading and handing it back to me. "Sir, this is crazy but I don't care what it says, it isn't my sister. She is dead and has been for over seven years."

"Do you know why someone would pretend to be your sister and attack her ex-husband's wife?"

"I don't know about his wife but I know, Todd deserves whatever he gets."

"Why would you say that?"

"Look detective, Todd is no saint. I don't know what he told you but he made my sister's life a living hell."

"I don't understand. He said it was the other way around and your sister was the one who had issues."

"Todd has a way with the truth. Let me show you something."

She gets up and goes into a room. After a few minutes, she comes out with two pictures. "Detective, this is a picture of my sister prior to meeting Todd and here she is afterwards."

"What happen to her?"

"Todd happened. I know Todd is living in Memphis with a new wife and son. He owns two restaurants and appears to be an upstanding citizen but he is anything but."

"Go on."

"My sister met Todd about nine years ago when she went to Memphis on business.

She worked for a pharmaceutical company and she traveled a lot. She and Todd started an affair. She would see him, the times she was in Memphis and he would come here."

"He told us the same thing."

"Anyway, their affair went on for about a year before my sister became pregnant. She had left her husband by then so it was no question whose baby she was carrying. Once there was a baby involved, she did not want to do the back and forth so she tried to break things off with Todd."

"Why?"

"He told her he didn't want a baby and she found out he was still married."

"He said he was going through a divorce."

"When Laylah was four or five months pregnant, Todd showed up on our doorstep with papers saying he'd finally divorced his wife."

"Did your sister believe him?"

"Of course because she was in love with him so when he said he was divorced, she agreed to marry him. They went to the courthouse two weeks later."

"What happened then?"

"Everything was going great. My sister was happy to be married and having a little girl. Then Todd's real wife showed up."

"Real wife?"

"There was never a divorce. I think my sister knew because somebody was sending her messages and leaving notes on her car but she believed Todd."

"What happened to the first wife?"

"After finding out about my sister, she went back to Memphis and divorced Todd, for real and never looked back."

"And Todd stayed here, with your sister?"

She nods. "Against our advice and pleas to leave him, she stayed. So, we shut up and began planning her baby shower. I'll never forget the date, May 24th 2011. The day I lost my sister."

She gets up and goes over to a drawer and comes back with a news article.

"Woman eight months pregnant, badly beaten after home invasion."

"There was no home invasion because whoever did this was in the house. No forced entry and the alarm was turned off. I know it was Todd but I couldn't prove it."

"He says he was in Memphis because your sister tried to kill him."

She chuckles.

"She never tried to kill him. Yes, somebody set their bedroom on fire but she was there too and could have been hurt. Fire officials investigated but could never find out who was responsible. After she was attacked, the police begin to dig into Todd's past and he ran. My sister laid in a hospital bed for three weeks, fighting to survive. The beating was so severe, it left her disfigured. The person who did it, stomped her in the stomach over and over until the baby was crushed."

"What happened to Todd?"

"He became Memphis' problem."

"Have you heard from him since?"

"Once, after the funeral when he came back to get the paperwork for her insurance. He couldn't even wait until her body was cold to cash in. I hope to never see him again, in this lifetime or the next."

"Thank you for your time."

"Detective, if Todd did this, stop him because he is a liar and a user. Get in touch with his first wife and she'll tell you."

"Do you have her name?"

"Aubrey Daniels. She was young and naïve but she knows his secrets. Find her and you'll see."

"Could she be the one doing this?"

She shrugs.

"Could it be you?"

She smiles.

"Is it you?" I ask her again.

"What would I have to gain by attacking his wife?" She asks.

"You can make him pay for taking your sister"

"Yea, I can also blame God but you don't hear me cursing Him, do you? Detective, if it were me, I wouldn't go after his wife because it would be Todd I'd torture. So before you start to suspect me, maybe you should check your source. Todd is not who he portrays to be. Now if you are done, I have work to do."

I stand to walk out.

"One last question. Was your sister dealing with mental issues from being attacked in college?"

"Hell no. My sister was attacked but she dealt with it, through counseling and her passion for photography. That's a lie Todd tells to keep folk from looking at him."

"Thank you again and I apologize for bothering you."

"Oh and detective, you didn't have to come all this way because a phone call would have sufficed."

"You're right but I needed to see for myself."

"Well, she's buried in Guthrie Cemetery, plot number 3275, if you need any more proof. Or you could have easily pulled her death certificate. I know Todd is a smooth talker but I'll be damned if I let him bad mouthed my sister, in death."

"I didn't mean to upset you."

"Then you shouldn't have come."

When I get to the car, I hear Kaylah's voice in my head. *"Check your source. Todd is not who he portrays to be."*

"How does Grant Nelson fit in? What about Octavia?" I ask talking to myself. "What in the hell is going on?"

I grab my phone to call my partner, Detective Tim Warren.

"What's up Collins, are you back in Memphis?"

"Not yet but have you heard anything on Octavia Wright?"

"Nawl man, we haven't located her yet. Her phone is off so we can't trace it. There hasn't been any credit card usage and the OnStar is disabled on her vehicle. We have someone checking her apartment but it doesn't look like she has been there for almost a month."

"What about family?"

"Uh," he says sounding like he's shuffling papers. "She has a cousin who lives in Jackson Mississippi but she hasn't heard from her either."

"Thanks man."

"Is everything okay?" He asks.

"No, something isn't right about this entire case but I cannot figure it out."

"Anything I can do until you get back?"

"As a matter of fact there is. Can you to pull everything you can on Todd Patrick, Laylah Patrick, Kaylah Gilmore, Grant Nelson and Aubrey Daniels because something isn't adding up?"

"Will do."

"Thanks. I'll be in when I touch down."

Rylee

"Hey, how did you sleep?" Rae asks when I walk into the kitchen.

"I didn't and why are you still here when you have a husband at home."

"He knows where I am."

"Raegan, I don't need a babysitter."

"Who said anything about babysitting you? I am here because I am worried about the psycho that's on the loose."

I sigh.

"Where's TJ?"

"I had Maribel take him to her house."

"Why?"

"Because we need to figure out what the hell is going on. I've been doing some research on Laylah." She said turning the computer around.

"Let me grab some coffee first."

I fix a big cup of the strongest coffee I have before joining Raegan in the living room.

"What did you find?"

"Her obituary." She says pushing the computer to me.

I begin to read out loud.

"Laylah Patrick, 36 of Charleston, SC died on May 24th, 2011. She loved photography, traveling the world and capturing the happiness of those around her. Her camera flashed, one last time as she was taken from this world, along with her daughter Trinity. She will be greatly missed by her only sister Kaylah Gilmore, other family members and friends. A memorial service will be held at a later date."

"Wow, this is sad."

"Something isn't adding up Rae."

"What do you mean?"

"Why would someone pretend to be her and she has been dead seven years?"

"Do you think it could be her?"

"It's not possible but somebody is going through a whole lot of trouble to make us think it is."

"Why though, after all this time and why go after you and not Todd?"

I shrug and begin typing on the computer. "Here's an old news report."

I press play.

"Local woman, Laylah Patrick who was viciously attacked in her home has died. Many held out hopes she'd survive but her sister has confirmed, this Memorial Day Weekend, she has succumbed to her injuries. As you may know, Laylah Patrick was eight months pregnant when she was badly beaten in her home. Members of her family tell us it happened the morning of her baby shower. Sources close to the investigation say the attack was so severe, the baby was crushed in her abdomen. Police are offering a ten thousand dollar reward for any information on the attacker."

I stop the video.

"Oh my God Rae! Is it possible Todd would kill her and the baby? Why though? What's the motive?" I ask.

"Girl, don't you watch the ID channel? Money is always the motive. How else would he be able to open the restaurants?"

"He said his parents -- I need to call Todd."

"What? Why are you calling Todd when he could be the one behind all this?"

"To see if he will tell the truth." I say jumping up. "Where is my phone?"

"Let me call it." She shakes her head. "It's going straight to voicemail."

"Dial his number from your phone."

She dials it and put it on speaker.

"What's up Raegan, is everything okay?"

"Did you kill Laylah?"

"Rylee? What are you talking about?"

"Did you kill her and her baby?"

"No, I would never do anything like that."

"Then why all the lies."

"It was easier than the truth."

"What is the freaking truth? The least you can do is be honest, with me, when it is now my life on the line."

He sighs. "Truth is—hold on." He says.

"Todd? Hello?"

"Rylee, let me call you back."

When he hangs up, I hear the email notification. I sit on the couch.

"It's an email from the "real forgotten wife." I say using air quotes.

"What does it say?"

To: Forgotten Wife

Subject: RE: The Forgotten Wife

Man, it is fun playing with you. I guess you know by now my name isn't Laylah. Yes, Todd was married to a Laylah but I am not her. Who am I? You will find out soon enough. Why now? You will find that out too. I have to commend you, though, you are one strong chick because I didn't think you would respond, again, after that beating you took.

I guess Grant's soft ass couldn't go through with it. No worries because there is always a next time.

So, I'll be in touch because we both know your sister will not always be there.

Until next time,

--

"There is no name this time."

"Who do you think it is?"

"Rae, I have no idea but whoever he or she may be, they are watching me."

Todd

I sigh, "Truth is—hold on."

"Todd? Hello?" Rylee says.

"Rylee, let me call you back."

I end the call when I hear someone moving inside. I push open the door and see my computer is on but the room is dark.

"Who's there?"

"Just the person I have been waiting on."

"What are you doing here?"

"Tying up some loose ends."

"What loose ends?"

"I had to respond to your wife's email, from your computer. See, when the police investigate, they will see you have been the one sending the emails all along."

"Why would I need to send Rylee emails pretending to be someone else?"

"Because it will show how demented you really are. I have to give her credit though. She is a ballsy chick. I thought after that beating, she would back down."

"It was you?"

"Of course. All part of the plan."

"What plan?"

"My plan of revenge."

"Revenge? For what?"

"For what you took from me."

"And what was that?"

"Not what, who?"

"Who then?"

"Laylah."

"Laylah? All of this is about her? She's dead."

"She's dead because of you, which means you owe me."

"Look, this game is getting old and I am sick of the back and forth. So either tell me what you want or get out."

"Fine, I want you. It's only fair, life for a life."

I open my eyes and realize I am looking up at a ceiling. I try to move but I can't. My hands are tied, in front of me. I reach for my head and when I pull my hand back, there is blood.

I blink a couple of times to get my eyes to focus clearer before trying to move again. I finally sit up, next to a wall and the pain in my head increases.

"Hello," I cringe. "Is anybody there?"

Silence.

"Hello. Where am I?"

My legs are also bound at the ankles.

"Hello!"

More silence.

I blink some more and that's when I notice a wall covered in pictures of me and my family. I try to stand but the pain …

Detective Hunter Collins

"Warren, you find something?"

"Man Collins, did you get any sleep last night?"

"I tried but there is something not adding up about this case. I've been up most of the night."

"Well, I don't think its Octavia."

"Why do you say that?"

"This chick posted to social media, faithfully but stopped about a month ago. She hasn't used her bank card and nobody has heard from her. I'm telling you Collins. She is either on the run or she's dead."

"What about her car?"

"It's a 2017 Yukon Denali but I can't locate it. OnStar tried, a couple of weeks ago but it was disabled."

"Can you check it now?"

"Can't hurt." He says. After thirty minutes, he slams down the phone. "Bingo! You're not going to believe where her truck is parked."

"Where?"

He slaps a piece of paper down on the desk.

"Wait, this is -"

"Yep."

"Let's go and see if you can get us a warrant in route."

Twenty minutes later, Detective Warren and I pull up to the restaurant, Lilies 2. A few other police cars meet us there and are parked in front of the truck.

"Guys, we have a warrant for this truck and that restaurant. We are looking for one, Octavia Wright, who is the owner of the truck and Todd Patrick, the owner of the restaurant.

Detective Warren, you search the truck while I go inside the restaurant."

I walk around to the back and bang on the door labeled as delivery.

After a few minutes, the door opens.

"May I help you?"

"My name is Detective Clinton Collins with the Memphis Police Department. Is Todd Patrick here?"

"No but I'm the general manager Ramon Vaugh. What's going on?"

"I have a search warrant for the premises."

"Search warrant? What are you looking for?"

"I'll tell you when I find it. Have you spoken to Todd today?"

"Not this morning but it looks like he was here earlier."

"Why do you say that?"

"Because there is some stuff out of place in the office."

"What kind of stuff?"

"Some papers thrown around and the computer is on."

"Can you show me?"

I follow him back to the office. "Is this computer ever left on?"

"Not usually."

I put on gloves and sit at the computer. Shaking the mouse, "Well I'll be damn!"

I stand up from the desk.

"Sir, are there cameras facing the parking lot?"

"Yes. Click on the security icon. Do you need me to show you?"

"I got it. This officer will take you outside while we conduct a search of the premises. On your way, call Todd and tell him to get here."

I open the security app and search through the cameras. When I locate the one I need, I rewind it back and press play. After a few minutes, I watch as the truck pulls in, parks and the door opens.

"Shit!" I say when I cannot make out the face of the person driving.

"Collins, there was nothing we could physically see in the truck. It looks to have been wiped cleaned." Warren says on the radio.

"Have crime scene go through it to make sure there isn't anything hiding."

"Will do."

I try a few more of the cameras but I still cannot see who it was driving the truck. It could be Octavia dressed in disguise and then again, it can be anybody.

"Collins, we got something in the kitchen." An officer says.

"I'll be right there."

I go up front and instruct a crime scene technician to have someone pull the footage from the security camera before walking over to the freezer door.

"What we got?"

"This way."

At the back of the freezer, I stop in my tracks. "Mother- Dispatch, we got a 187 at my location. Roll the coroner."

Rylee

"Give me that computer." Rae says.

"What are you doing?"

"Something I should have done a long time ago, a search on Todd."

"I've tried and nothing came back."

"Well, I have some resources for when we hire at the church. What's his social security number and date of birth?"

"447-00-9809 and November 17th 1976."

"Give me a minute." She says.

"How could I miss this Rae? How could I not know the man I have spent the last six years of my life with?" I ask her. "And I had the audacity to be angry he'd forgotten me. Hell, forgetting probably saved my life."

"Rylee, we don't know what all this means yet."

'Yes we do. It means I am married to a liar, cheater and who knows what else."

"Here we go. I found Todd's first wife's name. It's Aubrey Daniels."

"Is she still alive?" I ask.

"I don't know? Why does it matter?"

"Who knows? Maybe she is the one behind this or she can tell us more about Todd."

She goes back to the computer, tapping on the keypad for a few minutes.

"She's alive."

"How do you know it's her?"

"Her name is hyphenated on Facebook and she lives in Memphis. I'm about to message her."

"No Rae! We don't know if it's her."

"I guess we will find out because she's online."

Raegan starts to type, reciting out loud her message.

"Hey, you don't know me but my name is Raegan and my sister Rylee is married to your ex-husband Todd Patrick. I was wondering if we could meet to ask you some questions about him. We are willing to come to you, whenever you are available."

"Send!" She says.

"Well, at least he's not a serial wife killer." I say sarcastically. "Damn it! My husband could be a freaking killer."

"You don't know that so stop talking crazy."

"Really Rae? How would you be if this was your husband? I have a son with this man and he could be a killer. What if my son grows up-"

"RYLEE STOP!" She yells. "Look, I get you're upset but stop. Is Todd an asshole? Yes but we don't know all of the details so stop getting worked up."

"Whatever. I'm going to get a glass of wine."

"Rylee."

I keep walking as I hear her phone ring.

"Hey babe. Yea, I'm with her now." She snaps her fingers to get my attention. "No, what? Are you serious?"

"What?" I mouthed as she is trying to tell me something. "I.CAN'T.READ.LIPS." I say in slow motion."

"Let me call you back."

"What's wrong?"

"I was trying to tell you to turn on the TV." She barks. "Something happened at Lilies 2."

"Police say a body has been found in the freezer of Lilies 2 Restaurant and bar. We don't have much information, right now but sources say the body was found this morning when police came to investigate a truck in the parking lot. We have no word on who the deceased is but we will bring you more information when it becomes available. This is

Rose Carruthers reporting live for News Channel 23. Back to you."

"Oh my God!"

"Rylee calm down. You don't know if it's Todd. Call him."

"I can't find my phone."

"Here, use mine." She says handing it to me.

I dial Todd's number.

"He's not answering."

"Call Detective Collins."

I rush over to my purse and get his card. Dialing the number and put the phone on speaker.

"Detective Collins."

"Detective, this is Rylee. I just saw the news of a body being found at the restaurant. Is it Todd?"

"Rylee, where are you?"

"Home."

"I am on my way to speak to you."

"UGH!!!" I scream "What in the hell is going on?"

"Rylee, you don't know if it's Todd." Raegan says again.

"Would I be wrong if I want it to be?"

"Why would you say that?"

"Because maybe then all of this foolishness will stop. I'm going to take a shower and put on some clothes. Will you please call and check in with Maribel?"

Detective Hunter Collins

"Rylee, this is my partner Detective Tim Warren."

"It's nice to meet you." She says taking a seat in the chair. "Is it Todd?"

"No."

"Then who is it?"

"I cannot tell you until the body has been positively identified but I need to ask, when was the last time you talked to Todd?"

"This morning."

"Do you know where he was?"

"No, he abruptly got off the phone with after saying he'd call me back. Detective, what's going on?"

"I went to see Laylah's sister Kaylah, in South Carolina."

"Okay?"

"Todd admitted to the affair with Laylah but what he didn't mention was the fact, he wasn't divorced when he married her."

"Wow."

"Kaylah said somebody had been leaving messages and notes for Laylah regarding Todd but she wouldn't listen."

"What about the attempted murder?"

"Laylah wasn't responsible and Todd knew that."

"Well, he is great at lying."

"Kaylah said the same thing. Anyway, someone tipped off his wife, um her name is--" he says flipping through his notebook.

"Aubrey Daniels. We looked her up." Rae says.

"Yes. When Mrs. Daniels showed up and confirmed Todd's affair, she divorced him."

"Do you think she can be the one behind this and the emails?"

"Speaking of emails, they have been coming from Todd."

I don't say anything.

"You don't seem surprised Mrs. Patrick."

"They did know I had moved and that Raegan was here with me, so it makes sense."

"Do you also believe he is behind your attack?"

"I want to say no but he could have easily paid somebody."

"But why now? With Laylah, they were only together a few months before she was attacked. You two have been married for over six years. Why would he need to kill you now?"

"The affair."

"What affair?"

"I had an affair and when he found out he was livid. Oh my God, Liam."

"Who is Liam?" Rae asks.

"He's the one I had the affair with and he's dead."

"Wait, you had an affair with Judge Liam James?" Collins ask.

"Yes."

"Mrs. Patrick, do you have any idea where your husband could be? Any place he would go to hide out?"

"No. The only places I can think of are the restaurants."

"We know for sure he's not at either of them."

"Does he have any other properties?"

"Not that I know of but he is good at keeping secrets."

"Mrs. Patrick, I am not going to lie. This entire case is crazy but I made a promise to find out who is doing this and I will."

"Thank you detective."

We all stand.

"Wait, did you know Todd was suspected of killing Laylah Patrick?" I ask him.

"Yes but there was no proof."

"And? That doesn't mean anything when people have been convicted with a lot less." Rae says.

"You are right but until we have concrete proof, we cannot say Todd was responsible for her death. Rylee, I know this is a lot to take in and I wish I could give you answers to the questions swirling in your head but I can't, not at the moment. It is my hope, this will all be explained once I have located your husband. If you hear from him, call me."

When we get to the car, my cell phone rings with a call from the coroner. I answer and put it on speaker.

"What do you have for me doc?"

"I got a positive ID on your body. A one, Octavia Wright."

"Do you know how she died?"

"Asphyxiation."

"What about time of death?"

"Right now, I can't give you a definite time until the body thaws out and I finish the autopsy but a preliminary guess, she's been dead for weeks."

"So, she was frozen prior to being put in the freezer at the restaurant?"

"By all guesses, yes but I'll have more information for you in a few days."

"Thanks doc."

I hang up the phone and look at Warren.

"What are we missing? There is no way Todd had this body in the freezer, for weeks and nobody noticed."

"Not unless he had her stored somewhere else." Warren says.

"Has there been a record check to see if he has any other properties?"

"No."

"Then that's what we need."

"This means we are looking at a long night?"

"Yep."

Rylee

"Rae, go home to your husband."

"No, not until I know you are safe."

"Girl, I am grown and can take care of myself. Plus, I have security downstairs."

"What about TJ? Is he coming home?"

"No, Maribel is going to keep him until in the morning."

"Then come home with me."

"Raegan Haywood, I will not. Go home!"

"Why are you trying to get rid of me? It's not even that late."

"It's after nine and I just need some time to myself."

"Are you sure that's all it is? You're not going to look for Todd, are you?"

"And become his next victim, hell no! I am staying right here."

"Rylee, I know things are crazy but don't do anything to get yourself hurt. Let the police investigate."

"I am."

"If you need me, you better call." She says gathering her things.

"Yes ma'am."

After I send Raegan home, I go into the bedroom and find my phone in the covers on the bed.

I FaceTime Maribel to check on TJ but she doesn't answer. I go over to the dresser to get some pajamas.

Walking towards the bathroom, I hear my phone vibrating.

RAE: Old girl replied and said she wants no parts of Todd then she blocked me from her page.

ME: Wow. LOL!

RAE: Exactly but I'll do some more research and let you know what I find. Get some rest and I'll call you in the morning.

ME: I am headed to take a shower, a pain pill and then bed, mother!

RAE: I love you sister.

ME: I love you too.

I shower, oil my body down and change into my pajamas shorts and tank. Filling the glass, I had sitting on the sink with water; I turn off the light and walk out the door.

Taking two pain pills from the nightstand drawer, I swallow them before putting my phone on do not disturb. Sliding under the covers, I say a quick prayer and close my eyes.

But I can't fall asleep yet.

I decide to grab my computer from the living room. I get back into bed and open the top.

"Let me see what Google says."

I type in Grant Nelson.

"Too many. Hmm." I say tapping the keypad. "Grant Nelson + Memphis."

I scroll through a few things and nothing.

"Grant Nelson + South Carolina."

Grant Nelson opens Bistro in South's Carolina's downtown district.

I read through a couple of articles and then I see the obituary for his wife.

Yawn.

My eyes start to get heavy.

I click on the images tab of Google. Scrolling through all the pictures, I stop on one of Grant cutting the ribbon of the bistro. I sit up because the man standing behind him looks familiar but I cannot really see his face.

Clicking on the image, I am taken to the website of the local newspaper. The article is a few years old so I have to request access to see it.

I start filling in the information but I cannot stop yawning. I decide to finish it in the morning. I close the laptop and put it beside me on the bed and slide down under the covers.

Detective Hunter Collins

"Where do you want me to start looking?" Warren asks when we make it back to the station.

"See if Todd owns any other properties, in the city. Specifically somewhere that may have a freezer."

"On it."

"Something just isn't sitting right. Why kill Octavia and Judge James?"

"And what would have set Todd off now? His wife's affair?"

"We have seen husbands snap for less but all the pieces are just not fitting. Todd's ex-wife/girlfriend was attacked over six years ago. If he did it, he got away with it and received the insurance pay out. Wait, how was he able to marry Laylah when he was still married? Did he used another name?"

"Hmm, good question." Warren says typing. "No, he used the same name but a different birth year. The system never caught it."

"You mean to tell me, he's been that lucky? He buries one wife, comes back to Memphis, gets legally divorced, remarries and wait six years to try and murder his new wife?"

"Not to mention Grant Nelson."

"Did we ever get the background checks back?" I ask Warren.

"Yeah, hold on." He moves some paperwork around until he finds a thick envelope. Opening it, he starts to read out loud.

"Aubrey Daniels lives here in Memphis. She is a nurse at St. Francis Bartlett. It looks like she married Todd, right after high school. She has filed bankruptcy twice but she doesn't have a criminal record. She is remarried with three children. Her husband is in the military and stationed overseas."

"Nah, keep going." I say.

"Kaylah Gilmore is squeaky clean. Never been married, no children, not even a parking ticket. She works from home for Amazon, her finances seem to be in order and she has lived in South Carolina all her life."

I shake my head.

"Grant Nelson was from South Carolina. Married once to Gina Nelson. He was doing great financially, no debts, a few speeding tickets but no criminal record. He opened a Bistro Café, a year after his wife died. There is another man's name on the deed. It's Sampson Montague."

"Sampson? Why does that name sound familiar?"

I look at Warren and wave for him to continue while I figure out that name.

"Laylah Gilmore was born in South Carolina. She worked for a pharmaceutical company. She was married in 2007 and divorced in 2010. She and Todd went to the courthouse in January of 2011 but we know it wasn't legal. She was attacked, May of that same year."

"Does it say who her first husband was?

"Yea, his name was – hol-lee shit!"

"What?"

"Look." He says showing me a picture. "Isn't that the dude?"

"Hell yes, it is. Put out an APB. I need to call Rylee."

"You don't think he would go after her, do you?"

"If he is the one behind this, then he is also the one who had her attacked the first time. Let's go."

"Wait," Warren says, "We need to find out more information on him. It'll take thirty minutes, max."

"We may not have thirty minutes."

"But we cannot go off halfcocked Collins, we need to know who we are dealing with."

"Fine, you run that while I try to get a hold of Rylee or her sister."

Todd

My eyes pop open when water is thrown in my face.

"Good, you're up."

Looking around, the fuzziness clears and I remember where I am. I try to move but I am tied to a chair.

"Hello, are you with me?" He asks slapping me on the face.

"Why are you doing this?"

"Me? No, this has been all you."

He presses a button and the news begins to play on the TV.

"An update on the continuing news story. Investigators were at the scene of Lilies' 2 Restaurant and Bar for most of the day after a body was found in the freezer, earlier this morning. Police have not released the name of

the deceased but sources, close to the investigation, believes it to be a woman."

The TV is shut off.

"Whose body is that?"

"Octavia." He laughs.

"You killed her?"

"She was becoming a problem." He says rubbing the blade of a knife. "She saw me watching y'all, the night your wife was attacked. I knew it was only a matter of time before she told you and I couldn't have that. I sent her a text, pretending to be you and she fell for it. When she showed up at my house, we had sex and I killed her."

"Where has she been all this time?"

"A freezer in my garage."

"Why put her body at the restaurant now?"

"Because things are coming to an end."

"Where am I?"

"You don't recognize this place?"

I look around and shake my head.

"This is the house you lived in, while you were having an affair with my wife."

"You were married to Laylah?"

"I was until you took her from me."

"What are you talking about?"

"STOP ACTING CRAZY!" He says slicing me across the jaw with the knife.

"AH!" I scream as blood stains my shirt. "Why are you doing this? What do you want?"

"I want you to pay for taking her from me."

"I didn't take her from you."

He stabs me in the left knee.

"Ah, stop! Please."

"I will stop when you stop lying."

"Just tell me what you want." I cry. "Please."

"I want my life back. The life YOU TOOK!"

He stabs me in the arm.

"Please stop!"

"Please stop." He mocks. "We were happy and in love and I thought I was doing everything right. Then she said, I forgot her. She called herself The Forgotten Wife." He says putting air quotes around it. "But I didn't forget her, I was trying to provide."

"Why drag Rylee into this? She didn't even know me then."

"She's collateral damage."

"Don't hurt her. She has nothing to do with this."

"That's where you're wrong. She has everything to do with this."

"How, when I didn't even know you were married to Laylah? She told me her marriage was over because her husband didn't love her anymore."

"I DID LOVE HER! I just forgot to show it."

"Why is that my problem?"

He grabs me by the neck.

"It became your problem when you started screwing her."

When he releases me, I start coughing.

"I didn't know."

"You didn't care either. Every time she came to Memphis, she would lay up in this house, with YOU!"

"Look, I--" cough, "I was going through a rough time in my marriage and I was in a different state of mind but I am not the one to blame. She's the one you were married too. Not me!"

"You're right but no matter how I tried to get her to see you for the cheating bastard you were, she never would."

"It was you sending her the notes?"

"Yep but she still wanted you. Even after everything I did, from telling your wife to setting the bedroom on fire, she still didn't believe me. That's why she had to pay too."

"If she meant so much to you, why did you have to kill her?"

"I didn't plan to hurt her, all I wanted was for her to talk to me. I asked her to give me another chance but she laughed in my face. She said I wasn't man enough because you gave her the one thing I couldn't, a baby. While she stood there, smiling and rubbing her belly; something inside of me snapped."

"Why kill my baby?"

"Because she was yours."

"You're sick!"

"I couldn't stand to see her carrying another man's seed."

"Why pin it on me?"

"You made it easy with all the lying. When you took the first plane back to Memphis with a big insurance check, it only made the police more suspicious."

"There was nothing left for me there. I came back home, started over and met Rylee."

"I know."

"So this entire time, you have been plotting your revenge one me?"

"Yep, for eight years. Two thousand, nine hundred and twenty days. I used to lay awake at night, tasting your blood."

"Why did it take so long?" I laugh and then groan in pain. "You couldn't find the courage?"

"Nawl, it was never about courage, I was just away for a while."

"In a crazy house, I hope."

"Something like that."

"That can't be true because I ran your background check."

"You ran *a* background check." He laughs. "At first, I thought you had changed and was no longer the asshole you were before but you couldn't keep your dick in your pants. Even after I tried to warn you of your wife's affair."

"You already knew about the affair?"

"I know everything about you and her. I've watch your every move for the last year. It was really easy too. All I had to do was install a few small cameras in your house, cars and offices and clone your phone."

He steps back and pulls a phone from his pocket.

"What are you doing with my phone?"

"I'm not doing anything but you are telling your wife goodbye. See, I had plans to kill you, right after Laylah but I got caught up in some stuff."

I watch him as he types.

"When I was sent to prison, I spent every waking moment thinking about you. While my cellmates were being visited by their wives and children, I had nobody."

He types something else.

"I envied you. You moved on like Laylah didn't exist. You started a new life and you're happy. YOU DON'T GET TO BE HAPPY!"

He types something else.

"Six years of happiness with Rylee is enough. Don't you agree Todd?"

Just then a noise is heard outside.

"HELP!" I scream causing him to punch me in the face.

Rylee

I feel a hand on my face so I jump up.

"Rylee, it's me."

"Rae, what the hell?"

"You had us worried."

"Who is us?"

"Me and Detective Collins."

"What's going on?"

"Put some clothes on and meet us in the living room."

"What time is it?"

"4:30am."

I throw the cover back and get up.

"You couldn't call first?"

"We've been calling for the last two hours."

"Shit! I took a pain pill and put my phone on do not disturb."

I walk into the closet and throw on some jeans and t-shirt.

When I get to the living room, all of them turn to face me.

"What's going on?"

"Have a seat."

"Y'all are scaring me. Just tell me, is it Todd?"

"We know who is behind this?"

"Who?"

He hands me a piece of paper.

"Wait, this is Ramon, Todd's head chef."

"His real name is Sampson Montague. He was married to Laylah."

"Wait, what? Is he the one who was sending the emails?"

"Seems that way."

"None of this makes sense. Have you all found Todd?"

"Not yet."

"Do you think he has him?"

"We don't know but it is a strong possibility."

"Why now?"

"According to what we've found, Laylah was married to Sampson when she began her affair with Todd. After they divorced, he was put into a court order mental facility, for eight months, after he beat a man in a bar fight." Collins states.

"We believe, once he was released, he went back for Laylah but she was pregnant and involved with Todd." Warren interjects. "I was able to speak to a counselor and she states, all he talked about was getting her back."

"And nobody thought to look into him until now?"

"No. They had no reason to suspect him because they were divorced."

"Didn't the therapist have a duty to warn her of him?"

"We don't know."

"Well, where in the hell has he been since then?"

"We are investigating that now. It's possible he was locked up again or simply waiting until the right time to make his move."

"Make his move? For what? I still don't understand what this has to do with me."

"We don't either but I am waiting on his full record to be sent over. Maybe we can find something, he left behind that can give us some insight into why he is hell bent on destroying you and Todd."

"What am I supposed to do in the meantime?"

"I want to place you into protective custody until we have him."

"Oh my God, TJ." I run to get my phone.

I snatch it off the nightstand and when I unlock it, I see four text messages from Todd.

TODD: Riley, I didn't mean for this to happen. Please forgive me.

TODD: I didn't mean to kill Octavia but she deserved it.

TODD: Take care of my son for me.

TODD: I love you.

"Rylee, what's wrong?" Rae asks when I walk slowly down the hall.

"Uh, I got some texts from Todd's phone but they are not from him."

"How do you know?"

"For starters, he spelled my name wrong. And these sound nothing like him."

"Warren, call and see if we can trace the phone. Rylee, reply and see if you get a response. If the phone is still on, we can find out where it is."

"Okay."

ME: Todd, where are you? I'm worried about you.

Todd

I open my eyes to see him watching a video of Rylee.

When I moan, he turns to me.

"Are you going to act right now?"

"Is that live?"

"Nah, I never got the chance to install cameras at her condo. I have been there though."

"Were you the one who sent those photos?"

"Yes, they were some great shots too. I thought the pictures would make you go home but when you laughed about it, that day at the restaurant, I knew it was time to make you pay. I mean, you got pictures of your wife screwing another man and you still didn't do anything to save your marriage."

"My marriage is none of your business. If I wanted to screw every woman on the planet, it's my right and killing me isn't going to change that or bring Laylah back."

"You're right but I'll get to console your grief stricken wife. I'll be the one holding her at night and making love to her, when she's ready. And damn, she's sexy. I watched her have sex with that man and the way she moans when she has an orgasm. Damn! How could you forget that?"

"You're a psycho!"

He laughs. "The last dude said the same thing."

"What dude?"

"The one she had the affair with. He started getting pushy, demanding that she see him so I had to take care of him too. I didn't need him ruining my plans."

"What about your wife?"

"She's dead, remember."

"So, you aren't married?"

"Hell no. I only told you that so you would trust me."

"The church--"

"Another lie. Man, do you think God cares about someone like me? Fuck no but I am not looking to be saved."

"You are crazy."

"So I've been told."

"Rylee will never go for this. She will never go for you."

He laughs. "I wouldn't be so sure."

Just then my phone vibrates. I watch him unlock it.

"How do you know my code?"

"I know everything about you. Aw, your wife is worried about you." He says holding up the phone. "She wants to know where you are. Should I reply and say, on your deathbed?" He laughs.

"Leave her out of this."

"What are you going to do? Save her?"

He stabs me in the stomach.

"Are you going to save her boss man?"

I cry out from the pain.

"You should have listened when I told you to leave Octavia alone and go home but no, you had to have her. You had a wife at home who was begging for your attention and you forgot her."

I cough and then laugh.

"The same way you forgot Laylah. That's why she came to me. You were not man enough for her but I made sure to give her everything she needed, when she was in my bed."

"SHUT UP!"

"She was good at it too. Man, I remember the way she used to suck--"

He begins stabbing me, over and over.

"SHUT UP! You don't get to talk about her."

I spit blood onto his shirt.

"I'll never let you have my family."

"Good thing I won't need your permission."

"FUCK YOU! You crazy bastard! I hope you burn in hell."

"I probably will but not before you. Don't worry, I am going to put you out of your misery and I can promise it will hurt."

He walks behind me and pulls my head back. "Save me a spot in hell," He whispers in my ear before slowly dragging the knife over my throat.

Rylee

"He responded. It says, you don't have to worry about me anymore."

I look up at Collins who is looking at Warren.

"Got it. The phone is pinging at a house on Maple Valley Cove."

"Rylee, I am going to have an officer take you and your sister to the station. At least you will be safe there."

"What about my son?"

"I'll send a car to get him and the nanny and bring them to you."

I turn to walk into my bedroom but then I stop.

"No."

"No? What do you mean?" Rae asks.

"I am tired of being scared. What's to say he hasn't killed Todd already? No, I am not leaving."

"Rylee, don't be silly. There is a maniac on the loose who has attacked you once."

"Even more reason not to run. I say we get him to come to us."

"Hold on," Collins says. "I am not willing to jeopardize your life. He could already be headed here."

"Or he's not."

"Rylee, this is a bad idea. Think about TJ."

"I am thinking about him. Rae, if this man gets away, I will never feel safe again."

"I think you are making a big mistake." She says.

"I understand and I value your opinion but what if this was your life? Would you want to have to look over your shoulder for the rest of it?"

"Rylee, we can get him." Collins says.

"You might but it's a crap shoot. Right now, he is texting with me and he doesn't know I have figured out it's not Todd. All I have to do is tell him to come here. When he shows up, you grab him."

"It sounds easy but there is always a 50/50 chance something can go wrong."

"I'm willing to take that chance. So, I am going to go and put on some tennis shoes. Detective Warren, make a call for my baby to be picked up, Detective Collins set up whatever needs to be and Rae, go home."

I don't even give them chance to respond before I turn and go back to my bedroom. Sitting on the end of the bed, I let out a heavy sigh and say a quick prayer to God and open my phone to text Ramon.

ME: Todd, I am worried about you. Come here and let's talk. We can figure this out.

I lay the phone down and go into the closet to put on shoes. I come out, still no response.

I text again.

ME: Todd, baby please. You are scaring me.

While I wait, I call Maribel. After a few rings, she answers.

"Mrs. Rylee, what's wrong?"

"Maribel, I am so sorry to call you at this hour but a police officer is on the way to your house to take you and TJ to the police station. I don't want you to panic but can you please be ready? I would not ask if it were not for your safety."

"Yes ma'am, we get ready now." She says, her Spanish accent heavily coming through.

"Thank you and I will see you soon."

Releasing the call, I open the Message app.

Still no response.

"Has he answered?" Collins asks when I walk back into the living room to see Rae still here.

I shake my head.

"Then we need to get you out of here."

"A few more minutes and if he doesn't reply, I'll go with you."

I pace around the room, constantly looking at the phone.

"Rylee--"

"I know Rae. Let's go."

I grab my purse and keys. We get downstairs and Detective Warren instructs the officer to transport us to the station.

"Rylee, I've already briefed my captain. He will have someone waiting for you and your family when you arrive."

"Detective, please stop Ramon and save my husband."

"I will do my best. Stay safe."

"You too."

I lay my head back on the seat as tears begin to fall.

"Rae, why would Ramon do this? I only met him once but he seemed nice."

"Baby, there are a lot of wolves dressed like sheep. We may never know why he did what he did but we will get through it. Okay?" She grabs my hand.

When I see her bow her head and close her eyes, I know she's praying so I close mine as the tears continually fall.

We ride, without talking, for over twenty minutes with the only noise coming from the officer's radio. Pulling up to the station, we hear a frantic call ...

"SHOTS FIRED, OFFICERS NEED ASSISTANCE TO 5541 MAPLE VALLEY COVE. I REPEAT, SHOTS FIRED, OFFICERS NEED ASSISTANCE."

Hours later

We've been moved to a hotel room. Maribel and TJ are in the bedroom and Rae and I are in the living room. She is asleep on the couch and I am looking out the balcony door.

I hear a key slide in the door.

I jump up.

"Rylee, its Detective Collins."

"Detective, did you get him?"

"We did. He's dead."

"What about Todd? Where is he?"

"Rylee, I'm sorry but he was already deceased."

"NOOOOO!"

Raegan

TWO DAYS LATER

"Rylee, you don't have to do this. I can have the coroner bring you a picture to identify his body." Collins says as we walk through the doors of the morgue.

"No, I need to see him."

"Sister, are you sure?" I ask rubbing her back as she grips my husband, Nathan's arm.

"Yes, I'm sure. Please stop asking me that!" She yells.

"Have a seat and I will let Dr. Chanter know we are here."

She sits and her leg is shaking so fast. I place my hand on top to stop it. She closes her eyes and takes in a deep breath as tears fall.

"Lord, give strength now. We know you are able and at this moment, we need you like never before. Please oh God, we need strength. Amen." I pray.

I look at her and smile.

"Rylee, we are ready."

We walk into the cold, gray room. The medical examiner is standing on the opposite side of the table. Detective Collins is holding the door open.

"Mrs. Patrick, I am going to pull the sheet down, just below your husband's chin. I need you to prepare yourself. Are you ready?"

She is staring at the sheet.

"You ready?" I ask, touching the small of her back.

She jumps.

"Yeah." She whispers, wiping her face.

When he pulls the sheet back, Rylee lets out a scream that could rattle glass.

"What did he do to you?" She cries, rubbing his face. "Oh my God. Why did this happen?"

"Mrs. Patrick, is this your husband?" Dr. Chanter asks.

She shakes her head.

"Yes, it's him. It's my husband."

She stands there for another few minutes. Nathan touches her arm and she steps back. When he sees her swaying, he reaches for her and she passes out.

Rylee

I open the door to Detectives Collins and Warren.

"Rylee, how are you holding up?"

"To be honest, I don't know. These last few days have been a blur." I say walking them into the living room. "Can I get you something to drink?"

"No thanks."

"Have a seat."

No one says anything for a few minutes.

"The coroner finally released Todd's body to the funeral home you selected."

"I know, they called this morning. Detectives, did you all find out why Ramon, Sampson or whatever his name did this?"

Collins looks at Warren.

"What?"

"We received this, last night, from the South Carolina Parole Commission." He hands me a huge folder.

"Apparently, Sampson was serving time in prison, up until a year ago, for vehicular manslaughter. Upon his release, he dropped off the face of the earth and became Ramon Vaugh. Brace yourself because some of the things you are about to see are demented."

I take the folder and open it. The first thing I see is a sheet of paper in plastic with the words, The Forgotten Wife, written in big bold, red letters.

"Is this blood?"

"We think so."

I flip to another page and its newspaper clippings about the attack on Laylah and her obituary. In all of them, her face is scratched out.

"Nobody found this strange?"

"The thing is, these items weren't discovered until he'd been released. They were found in a hole, behind the bed he was sleeping in. Once they were located, officials turned them over to the parole commission but nothing was ever done because Sampson Montague dropped off the face of the earth."

"So they wash their hands of it instead of trying to find him?"

"It looks that way."

I shake my head and continue to flip to see pages of handwritten notes on Todd. Pictures of Todd when he opened the restaurant, pictures of us together, from my Facebook page among other things. There is a journal. I flip it open.

"I don't even know what day it is but one things for sure, it's one day closer to my release. I can smell the air now. I wonder what it's like in Memphis. I don't know but I cannot wait to get there. I can already feel Todd's blood on my hands. The things I am going to do to him. Maybe I'll cut off his dick and send it to his wife. HAHA! Serves him right."

"Wow."

"The entire journal is like that."

"Where did he get all of this? The pictures and newspaper clippings?"

"From a pen pal he met while in prison. We've spoken to her."

"A woman? Did she have anything to do with this?"

"No. She is an older woman who is confined to her home. She get thrills from writing to men in prison and once he was released, she moved on to someone else."

"Okay, so he was out for revenge because he blamed Todd for taking Laylah. Where does Grant Nelson fit in?"

Warren speaks. "Grant and Montague shared a sexual relationship. From this, sparked the discussion of trading murders. When Montague held up his end of the bargain, Grant felt he had too much to lose if he didn't go through with it. We believe, he never had any intentions of having you killed but he needed Grant's hands to be dirty, along with his.

"With Grant attacking you, they each had something over the other. After the attack, we surmise Grant felt guilty and left the video before killing himself."

"All this over one woman?"

"Laylah wasn't just any woman to him, she was his soul mate. She was the one who grounded him and the only one who, in his words, loved every part of him. And seeing her with Todd, changed something within him."

"Did he kill her?"

Collins shakes his head yes.

"We also found evidence he'd been watching you."

"Watching me?"

"He had cameras in your house, office and car."

"Oh my God."

"There's more."

"Do I even want to hear it?"

"You will find out once you see the coroner's report and I don't want it to be a surprise to you. Todd's throat was cut but he didn't immediately die. Instead, he was tortured and castrated. He used his blood to write this on the wall."

He hands me a picture.

Thou Shalt Never Forget His Wife

"What does this mean?"

"I don't know. I guess it was a final dig at Todd."

"What about phones, videos or a computer? Did he leave anything else behind?"

"No. He destroyed the magnetic strips on all the hard drives and destroyed everything else. We were hoping to recover something, anything but we couldn't."

"All of this over a forgotten wife."

"It seems that way. Anyway, we will get out of your hair. I know times are hard right now but they will get better."

"Detectives, thank you for all of your hard work. You will never know how much this means to me."

Graveside Services

I sit in the chair, pulling on the ribbon that is around the flower. I see my sister standing at the head of the casket and although her mouth is moving, I cannot hear a thing she says.

I don't snap out of my thoughts until a young lady stands beside Rae and begins to sing.

"I can only imagine what it will be like, when I walk by your side. I can only imagine what my eyes will see, when your face is before me. I can only imagine. Surrounded by your glory, what will my heart feel? Will I dance for you Jesus or in awe of you be still? Will I stand in your presence or to my knees will I fall? Will I sing hallelujah, will I be able to speak at all? I can only imagine."

When the song is over, Raegan begins to speak as the funeral director motions for me to stand.

"To you, O Lord, we commend the soul of our dearly departed, Todd Patrick. Forgive whatever sins he may have committed and welcome him into your everlasting peace. For we count it all joy to know it has pleased our Heavenly Father, to take unto Himself our beloved. We therefore commit his body to the ground, earth to earth, ashes to ashes, dust to dust, looking for the blessed hope and the glorious appearing of the great God in our Savior Jesus Christ."

"You may now place your flowers."

"Jesus shall change the body of our shame into the likeness of His own body in glory, according to the working of His mighty power. When we shall see Him, we know it is well. Let us pray."

Someone begins to hum, Amazing Grace.

"God, our father in Heaven who is the giver, sustainer and taker of life; we thank you. God, we dare not question your motive but we thank you for the life of Todd and for the moments in time that are forever etched in our hearts. Now God, I ask for your comfort during the times we want to ask why. I ask you to wrap your arms around Rylee, signifying to her she is never alone. Give her rest on the nights her thoughts will not let her sleep. And God, when she cries, your words says in Psalm 56:8 that you bottle every tear and know of all our sorrows. Take them from her so they never weigh her down. For we trust you and it is in thy hands, God, I commit the life of your servant, saying it is well. Amen."

We all say amen.

"We, on behalf of Harrison Funeral Home, thank you for allowing us to serve your family during this most difficult time. We ask in the days, weeks and months to come; when the phone calls and visits stop, you will continue to pray for this family. If there is anything we can do for you now or in the future, please do not hesitate to call. You are now dismissed back to your cars."

A MONTH LATER

I walk to the door of TJ's room and watch him sleep. It has been a month since everything happened. I finally got TJ to sleep in his room and I think it was harder for me than him.

How have I been?

There are good and bad days AND nights. It is especially hard when TJ asks about Todd, all the time and I have explain why he hasn't been here.

Does a three year old really understand when you say, your dad is gone to heaven?

I placed a picture of Todd next to his bed and it seems to help. It breaks my heart when I walk in on him holding the picture or staring at it.

I am pulled from my thoughts by the vibrating of my phone.

RAUL: I sent you the image proof of the article. It looks amazing.

ME: Thank you. I will check it out and let you know.

I decided to write an article about The Forgotten Wife and some of the things I have gone through. I don't know if it will help anybody else but I have found journaling to be a great stress releaser.

Who knows, maybe I will turn it into a book.

I walk up front and get my computer from the counter before going into my bedroom. Getting comfortable on the bed, I take a sip from my glass of wine while the computer powers on.

Opening Outlook, I get ready to click on Raul's email but I hear a ding.

"Shit."

I sit the laptop on the bed and reach into the nightstand, pulling out a phone.

I open it and see an email.

From: Sampson

Subject: The Forgotten Wife

I know you are wondering why you're just getting this email but you can thank Microsoft Outlook for their delayed send feature.

Genius, right?

Anyway, I thought it only right you get this on the one month anniversary. Did you like the image, I left for you on the wall? I think it was a masterpiece, myself. What about you RILEY? LOL! I knew you would catch that in the text. Anyway, I don't have long because the police are outside my house but I could not leave without telling you something.

You're welcome.

-- Sampson.

P.S. No one will ever know you were my Stranger in the Bar.

I delete the email and smile before going into the laundry room.

Reaching under the cabinet, I grab the can of acid I'd hidden there for this occasion. I pop the seal on it and drop the phone in.

While I wait for the phone to sink, I think back to five months ago.

"Is this seat taken?"

"If you sit, it will be."

"What is a gorgeous woman like you doing at a bar, this time of night? Isn't your husband worried?"

"My husband is across the street, in those apartments with a woman he hired to work in our restaurant."

"Sounds like Todd."

"Wait, how did you know my husband's name?"

He slides me a picture of Todd and another lady. "I know more than you think Rylee. Your husband stole my wife."

I sit my drink down.

"So, what do you want?"

"Revenge."

"I'm sorry, what's your name?"

"Sampson."

"Well Sampson, what's in this for me?"

"A dead husband, if you play your cards right."

"What will I have to do?"

"Follow my instructions."

"I can do that."

"You might get hurt but you will not die."

"I can handle that too. What about you?"

"Oh, I will not make it out alive."

"And you're okay with that?"

"I am." He says.

"Then tell me more."

When I am satisfied with the phone being destroyed, I put the top on the can, place it in the back of the cabinet and turn off the light.

Walking back to my bedroom, I climb into bed and grab Todd's pillow. I smile while saying, "The 11th Commandment just might save your life. Thou Shalt Never Forget His Wife."

I hope you have enjoyed The Forgotten Wife. It is my first time writing a full mystery/suspense, so I hope I made you proud.

If you would, please leave a review and recommend it to your family and friends.

As always, thank you! Words cannot express what it means to me each time you support me!

If this is your first time reading my work, please check out the many other books available by visiting my Amazon Page.

For upcoming contests and give-a-ways, I invite you to like my Facebook page, AuthorLakisha, follow my blog https://authorlakishajohnson.com/ or join my reading group Twins Write 2.

Or you can connect with me on Social Media.

Twitter: _kishajohnson | Instagram: kishajohnson | Snapchat: Authorlakisha

Email: authorlakisha@gmail.com

About the Author

Lakisha Johnson, native Memphian and author of many titles was born to write. She'll tell you, "Writing didn't find me, it's was engraved in my spirit during creation." Along with being an author, she is an ordained minister, co-pastor, wife, mother and the product of a large family.

She is an avid blogger at kishasdailydevotional.com and social media poster where she utilizes her gifts to encourage others to tap into their God given talents. She won't claim to be the best at what she does nor does she have all the answers, she is simply grateful to be used by God.

Other Available Titles

A Secret Worth Keeping

A Secret Worth Keeping: Deleted Scenes

A Secret Worth Keeping 2

Ms. Nice Nasty

Ms. Nice Nasty: Cam's Confession

Ms. Nice Nasty 2

The Family That Lies

Dear God: Hear My Prayer

The Pastor's Admin

2:32AM: Losing Faith in God

Doses of Devotion

You Only Live Once: Youth Devotional

HERoine Addict – Women's Journal